Seeds of Destruction

By

Frances Bennett

Black Pear Press

Seeds of Destruction

Frances Bennett

First published in the UK 2014
By Black Pear Press
www.blackpear.net

ISBN 978-1-910322-06-2

Cover painting by Sheenagh Pearson
Cover design by Black Pear Press

This novel is entirely a work of fiction. The names, characters and incidents portrayed in it are the work of the author's imagination. Any resemblance to actual persons, living or dead is entirely coincidental.

Dedication

To my fellow writers at Worcester Writers' Circle, without whose encouragement this novel would never have reached the printed page.

Table of Contents

Prologue

The young man stood silently in the centre of the dim, high-ceilinged room listening to the measured tick of the grandfather clock in the hall.

How he had hated that sound. As a small boy the silence of the old house had borne down on him, smothering and stifling, the endless gloomy hours punctuated by that tick, tock, tick. The precise little valuer who had just left had told him it was one of the most valuable pieces in the house.

'A fine example, Mr Brown, very fine,' he'd sniffed. In fact he had sniffed constantly throughout his tour of the house, making his neat notes and sniffing. Almost as if scenting the air for bargains. He had been visibly excited by the furniture though considerably less so by the pictures.

'All Victorian, Mr Brown. No artists of real note but never mind; this is an interesting collection. I feel sure we shall get some excellent prices for you.'

He had shown a tendency to linger but was eventually ejected leaving one figure standing. The man had finally got rid of him and now he stood, in the silence, listening to the clock

He moved abruptly, making for the back of the house, the garden room. All the tools were arranged tidily, hanging on nails on the wall. He hesitated for a moment and then took down an axe, the one his grandfather's handyman had always used for splitting up the kindling for the fires they had burned in the huge old-fashioned grates. So many times he had stood and watched the rhythmic rise and fall of the shining blade, the satisfying thwack of metal into wood. He strode quickly up the hall and stood in front of the clock. Standing the axe against the banisters he moved to one side of the clock and heaved. It fell over with a jangling crash and the mechanism, jolted out of

1

time, started to strike. He lifted the axe and smashed it into the clock, the first few blows aimed carefully but eventually just hitting, bringing it down with stunning force, again and again and again until half an hour later there was nothing recognisable left, just a pile of splintered wood and bits of metal. Drenched in sweat and spent with effort the man went slowly upstairs to the shower, standing under the scalding needles for a long time. Dry and re-clothed he came down and painstakingly gathered every last piece of the shattered parts into a number of packing cases left by the removal company marked 'For Storage. Not to be opened.'

Searching for the longest nails he could find he hammered down the lids. Straightening he downed tools and walked to the centre of the drawing room, listening. The silence was total, complete.

After a few moments he mounted the three flights of stairs leading to the attics. Unlocking the narrow door he switched on the light, revealing a low-ceilinged room covered in a thin layer of pale dust. The air was stale and dry, smelling of age and disuse. The only furniture in the room was a big armchair and a large table. On the floor stood packing cases, some full, some empty. Patches of lighter colour on two of the walls were evidence of pictures removed but the other two were still covered with mounted photographs, some a single person, some a group of two or three. One face gazed out from every picture, a tall, slender laughing woman with a halo of chestnut hair and the background was always the same. Cliffs, sea and sand, an English coastal landscape of spectacular beauty.

The man started to work methodically removing the pictures and packing them carefully into the empty packing cases and sealing down the lids. By the time he finished the sun had slid behind the grey hills of Bath and dusk had crept into the attic. He straightened up from the last case and looked around, checking. Nothing left. He wrote the same instructions on the cases with a felt pen as on those downstairs and left, locking the door behind him. In the hallway he stood for a moment looking around, then left, slamming the heavy front door behind him. Getting into the scarlet Porsche parked at the curb he drove away without a backward glance. Behind him the old house settled into its silence again.

Chapter 1

The steady insect hum of a packed restaurant rose into the still night air, interspersed with sudden bursts of laughter and the slamming of car doors as people started to leave.

Comfortably wedged in the warm angle of the wall between the kitchen and dining room Tessa listened with weary satisfaction. Another successful Saturday evening almost over. She felt the taut muscles in her shoulders gradually relaxing against the sun-warmed bricks as sipping her coffee she watched her employer through the window. Chef's whites gleaming, tawny mane of hair falling away, Hester threw back her head and laughed, a sound and gesture familiar in thousands of sitting rooms throughout the country.

Tessa smiled to herself. What a performer she was. If she hadn't been a chef she would surely have been an actress. She worked the restaurant like a theatre or a catwalk.

Tessa flexed her back, wincing as she eased the aching muscles. It had been a long hard night and so hot. Time for a swim. She padded across the parched grass to the edge of the cliff and peered down at the sea, lapping silkily at the very foot. Better go now before the tide turned.

Lying on her back in the softly moving coolness she gazed up at the inky blackness studded with tiny points of light, the tensions of the evening gradually draining away as she floated, keeping herself buoyant with tiny movements of hands and feet. What a heavenly place this was and what luck getting a summer job here. The weather had been unbelievable too, more like Spain than England. She lay for a few minutes more then turned over and waded ashore. The dim expanse of the estuary stretched away, hazy and mysterious in the semi dark and suddenly she shivered and was surprised. It was still so hot and airless why should she suddenly feel chilled?

4

'Ridiculous,' she muttered, 'too long in the water.' Wrapping her towel around her already drying body she started up the path.

As she reached the top of the cliff Hester came to the door of the restaurant.

'Come on up to the flat and have a drink,' she called. Tessa was surprised. This was unusual. Normally Hester disappeared upstairs as soon as the last customer had gone, not to be seen again until mid morning next day.

'OK,' she called back. 'I'll just dump this wet stuff and I'll be there.' She went round the corner of the building into the garden at the back. The mobile home in which a succession of summer season chefs had been housed stood at the end, shaded by trees. Hester did not like to share her space with anyone, even temporarily, so this spacious caravan was ideal. Tessa slicked a brush through her wet hair, shrugged into shorts and a tee shirt, pegged out her swimsuit and towel on the line behind the van, and went back to the side entrance, which led to Hester's flat. As she entered the long sitting room she glanced round appreciatively. This was only her third visit. Hester guarded her privacy fiercely and most of their contact when not in the kitchen was in the restaurant where they sat every morning with a fresh jug of coffee planning and discussing the evening ahead. The living room was rectangular with windows all along one side overlooking the bay. Two huge sofas covered in creamy linen faced the view, scattered with bright cushions. The pictures were abstracts, patches of vivid colour on the white walls, with the one exception, a picture of Hester over the stone fireplace, caught exactly as Tessa had seen her earlier, head thrown back, laughing at the camera, standing at her kitchen table, chef's knife in one hand, glass of wine in the other. It was a hugely blown up photograph in a washed wood frame and it dominated the room. Tessa glanced at it with an inward grin as she sat down. She looked up to find Hester regarding her with very much the same wry amusement that she herself was feeling.

'Here you are,' she said putting a frosty looking glass on the sofa table. 'You think I'm a dreadful show off, don't you?'

Tessa smiled comfortably back at her. 'You'd hardly be the success you are if you couldn't promote yourself. I wish I had your confidence.'

Hester glanced sideways as she turned to sit down.

'Oh you'll get it, I've had to build mine.' She sat down opposite Tessa with her inevitable mug of coffee. Unusually for a chef, Hester rarely drank alcohol and ate very sparingly, which probably accounted, Tessa thought, for her excellent skin and figure.

Hester said nothing for some minutes, staring out at the dim outline of the bay. She seemed to have forgotten Tessa was there until the faint clink of the glass being replaced on the table roused her.

'Tess. I'm sorry. I was miles away. You must be wondering why I've got you up here so late, and after such an evening. My God, it was busy, but it went well, don't you think?'

'As always. Everyone seemed really happy.'

'Except that old misery on table five. I don't know why he keeps coming, nothing's ever right.'

Tessa chuckled. 'Do you think it might be a power thing? Maybe he likes to feel he's got a famous TV chef on the run. Particularly a woman. I think he's just that type, a typical RBR, silly old fool.'

Hester burst out laughing and in unison they chanted 'Rich Bored Retired!'

'You're absolutely right,' Hester said, 'I just hate complaints. I always feel undermined, it's so silly after all this time.' She put her empty mug on the table and leaned back in her chair regarding Tessa with a faint smile. 'You know I'm really enjoying having you working with me this summer. You're by far the best commis chef I've ever had. No one has ever supported me as well as you do, I just wish it was worth keeping you on permanently but the winters are so much quieter I can't justify it. You've probably got plans of your own, anyway.'

The slightly interrogative note in her voice required an answer but Tessa just smiled and said,

'Some, yes, but nothing settled yet.' She shifted in her seat. 'Well, if there's nothing else, I think I…' Hester interrupted her.

'I'm sorry, I'm sure you're completely shattered. It was just to let you know that my stepson will be here for three weeks as from tomorrow.'

'That would be Simon, would it?'

Hester looked astonished. 'How did you know?'

'I read that article about you in the Sunday Times a few months ago. You spoke of him.'

'So I did,' Hester replied thoughtfully. 'Well, you probably know that he is not strictly my stepson because I never actually married his father. We lived together for nine years and I did my best to fill the gap Simon's mother left. Poor kid, he really wasn't having much of a life.' She paused, staring out of the window.

Tessa didn't speak or move, just let the silence lengthen.

Eventually Hester continued. 'He was eleven when I came to live with Oliver. He came up to London from his grandfather's for a week at Christmas. Oliver went to meet him at the station while I waited at home. I was so nervous, afraid he wouldn't like me and for quite a long time I thought he didn't. He had this unnerving habit of coming into the room very quietly and just standing there as if he was waiting for something. Not saying a word.' She paused, remembering.

Tessa said thoughtfully, 'Perhaps if he lived on his own with his grandfather he got used to not saying much, you know, not speaking 'til he was spoken to. What was his grandfather like?'

'Oh, very old school, rigid and autocratic. Ex-Army but very fond of Simon. I think he just didn't know how to show affection. It was not something one did, particularly to a boy. Simon's mother was his only child and he was devastated when she died. She was only twenty-eight.'

'What happened?'

'She was in a car crash; she drove into a tree coming down from London late at night. No one knew why she was travelling down but it was thought she'd gone to sleep at the wheel. Simon was in the back of the car. It was a miracle he wasn't hurt, hardly scratched, but the car was a write-off.'

'So Simon went to live with his grand parents.'

'His grandfather. His grandmother was dead. Oliver was in a long run at the Shaftesbury and obviously couldn't look after him at that time. He was six. Anyway, Oliver is hardly the most responsible of people and an actor's life is not exactly conducive to child rearing.' Her voice was flat. Tessa sat quietly, watching her face. Some bitterness still there, she thought. How these feelings do cling on in the crevices of the mind.

'So how on earth did his grandfather manage?'

'He had a live-in housekeeper. She was all right but elderly too. You know the type; children should be seen and not heard. Simon was sent to prep school at eight and really only lived at home in the holidays. When Oliver was 'resting' he would have him up for a few days here and there but it wasn't 'til I came on the scene he could come regularly. He was so quiet and obedient he was unreal, but I dug him out of his shell eventually.'

'And he still comes for his holidays? Gosh, he must be how old now?'

'He's thirty-four. Yes, he comes for three or four weeks in the summer, a week at Easter and a few days at

Christmas until I close at New Year.'

'What does he do? I mean, not on holiday, the rest of the time?'

'He teaches, well, lectures actually at the LSE. He's been living with Oliver since we split up.'

'Not married?'

Hester grinned at her as she got up from her chair. 'No, and he's not gay as far as I can tell.' She paused as if she was weighing what to say, then slowly, 'There was one girl that…' She stopped and then continued more briskly, 'Well, I thought that it might have been permanent but it didn't come off.' She glanced at her watch. 'Anyway, I've kept you from your bed for long enough. He'll be here tomorrow staying in the spare room. He's quite useful around the place. He'll wait table or do the bar. He seems to enjoy it. Makes a change I suppose from teaching.'

As Tessa rose to leave, Hester added, 'Oh, his grandfather died in March. Left him everything. He must be quite a wealthy young man now.'

She twinkled at Tessa. 'You should try your luck, you could be just what he needs.'

Tessa smiled back. 'I don't think so. I do have other arrangements.' She ran down the stairs leaving Hester staring after her.

* * *

In the late afternoon of the following day the long scarlet car snaked in a wide sweep across the gravel at the back of the house crunching to a stop by the back door. Simon killed the engine and slumped back in the seat, eyes closed.

Not a sound. Yes, there was, but one so woven into the texture of the place that it was almost unnoticeable. The ever-present brushing whisper of the sea creeping up and back in the estuary. Motionless in the ticking warmth of the cooling car Simon's daylong headache began to recede.

9

At last, the maddening delays were over and he was here.

An ear splitting screech jerked him upright. An enormous gull perching on the bonnet glared at him over the menacing curve of its beak as if measuring him for dinner.

'Sod off!' he yelled and thumped the windscreen with his clenched fist. It didn't move, simply continued its contemptuous regard. Infuriated Simon punched the horn and it rose with a clatter leaving a glistening splodge across the windscreen as it flapped away.

'Bloody scavenger,' Simon muttered after it, flinging open the car door and yelping as his bare feet met the scalding gravel. He had forgotten kicking off his shoes for the last three miles down to the cove. He was groping for them under the seat when Hester's voice spoke from the back door.

'It had to be you, all that yelling and swearing. Obviously time you had your holiday. Come in and have a drink and calm down. Your luggage will do later.'

He straightened up to face her, tongue-tied as always at his first sight of her. Almost as tall as he, at six feet he only topped her by a couple of inches. Broad-shouldered and generous-hipped, apricot skin smudged with darker freckles, chestnut hair scraped back and tied with a scarf, she leant against the kitchen doorway, grey eyes gleaming with affectionate amusement.

His throat constricted. Almost he wanted that moment never to end. For a few seconds he was a child again, poised at the start of a summer holiday. Then she held out a hand and he was hugging her, breathing in the familiar scent of warm skin and sun oil, almost giddy from the rush of tension released.

She thumped his shoulder gently. 'Come on through. It's lovely under the willow.'

He followed her into the kitchen. It seemed nearly dark after the brilliance outside, heavy with the lush after-smells of cooking. Herbs and wine and garlic, sensuous reminders. Hester stopped by the towering refrigerator and removed an unlabelled brown bottle from the door shelf.

'Frank's still brewing then,' he commented.

'Brewing well. Seems better than ever this year.' They went down the narrow stone-flagged passage leading on to the terrace and Simon drew a deep breath. It never failed. Even after countless summers, stepping through that door, on to the warm stones, the view overwhelmed him.

Heavily wooded, the arms of the estuary swept majestically down on either side, shelving to shallow rocky scree that tapered into shimmering lemon-coloured sand. A huge pale expanse dotted with outcrops of grey rock and criss crossed with small runnels and streams and one long narrow wedge of water which never dried out but could be waded at low tide to reach the cove on the further side. Above the woods, silvery stubble fields flowed towards the horizon and ahead the sea spread out, a scarcely moving sheet of light blue silk, a cruiser sitting motionless, far out, tiny as a toy.

This was home as the crowded flat in London had never been, as the austere Bath crescent house of his grandfather had never attempted to be. The warm flags under his feet, the salty wind blowing soft and cool on his skin. This was home.

'Are you going to stand there all day?' Hester teased him. 'Come and sit down and tell me about everything.'

He crossed the terrace on to the scrubby grass and ducked under the willow branches where Hester lay on a padded garden chair, the wine bottle in a wine cooler and two gently fizzing glasses waiting on the iron table. He dropped into a chair and took a long swallow resting his head on the cushioned back, his eyes still turned seawards as if he couldn't tear them away.

From behind her dark glasses Hester studied him. As usual, she thought, tired out, strung up to snapping point and badly in need of rest and relaxation. I wonder if Tess might stir his interest but I doubt it. None of the summer girls ever had. Was he gay? No evidence either way except that dear Maurice at the pub had often lamented that he wasn't. 'Takes one to know one, sweetie.' Perhaps this time he would tell her that he'd found someone, though his domestic situation did make that rather difficult.

She realised he had spoken, but lost in her thoughts she had not heard what he had said. 'Sorry love, I was doing my usual. What did you say?'

He grinned at her. 'Calculating how many pounds you can put on me in the next few weeks, I suppose.'

'Something like that. Anyway, I'm concentrating now. Give me the gossip.'

The shadows were lengthening by the time Frank's bottle was upside down in the cooler and they had talked themselves almost to a standstill. Hester glanced at her watch.

'Six thirty. Time I went in. It's going to be a heavy one this evening.'

'Fully booked?'

'Yes and three tables double booked.'

'How's business?'

'It's held up very well all things considered. Some of the others are having a very hard time. You remember the couple at 'Hatchets' and the boys at 'The Galley?''

'Bust?'

''Fraid so. But they wouldn't change anything. They'd had it too good for far too long and by the time they started shedding staff and doing the work themselves it was too late. The banks pulled the plug.'

Simon stretched and yawned. 'Too easy to get slack

12

living down here. Lord knows how I'd get on. Still, maybe I'm about to find out.'

Hester had reached the side door, tray in hand. She turned and stared at him.

'Whatever do you mean?'

'Not sure yet. I want to talk to you but it'll keep. Are you still closing on Mondays?'

'Yes, that's my day off if you can call it a day off.'

'Well, perhaps I can come marketing with you and then we can have the afternoon and evening together. We've got a lot to discuss.'

She stood a moment longer, watching him, eyes narrowed and then gave a tiny shrug.

'OK,' she said setting off inside. She tried to keep her tone perfectly equable but she was irritated and he could probably tell. Why hadn't he broached whatever was on his mind during their conversation? 'Why don't you go for a swim,' she said, 'this weather may not last.'

Chapter 2

Monday dawned breathless and cloudless. Simon drew back the curtains and took a deep breath. Although it was still early the air was so warm that it took no imagination to realise by midday it would be baking. Swim now he decided. The tide would be half out already and it would be quite a walk down the estuary. Or perhaps the pool. Yes, he would go to the pool.

It had been the most magical part of the whole enchanting place when he was a child. Aunt Fliss had shown it to him on his first visit. A tongue-tied twelve year old. Hester had brought him down to meet her aunt. She had seemed old even then, gaunt and white haired and incredibly brown, dressed always in faded trousers and tee shirts and ancient stained canvas shoes. The only older people he had known previously were his grandfather and Mrs Thomas the housekeeper, his teachers at school and the few male friends his grandfather invited to the house. All old, upright and remote, they came to dinner with his grandfather and afterwards played bridge or chess. They would gravely shake his hand, make stilted conversation over pale dry sherry and then seem to forget he was there as he sat silently through the dull and tasteless three courses Mrs Thomas, equally silently, put in front of them. Not difficult to forget about him, he supposed, he didn't speak unless he was spoken to. It was safer that way. Aunt Fliss was a revelation. She seemed to enjoy his company. She would seek him out and gather him up and off they would go. He could still hear her voice:

'Come on Simon, stop frowsting away with that old book. We'll go crabbing.' That first holiday seemed to be a whirling kaleidoscope, every day something new and wonderful to explore and discover, and the most precious of all was the pool.

Aunt Fliss had come to his room early, on just such a

morning as this, and pulled back the curtains with a rattle.

'Come on, Simon, up you get. Put on your bathers, we're going to swim.'

He had looked out of the window and saw that the tide was out at its furthest point.

'It's going to be a jolly long walk,' he ventured. She had smiled down at him. 'It'll take us five minutes,' she said, 'come on, hurry up.'

Down the cliff path they had gone, he almost stumbling to keep up with her surefooted jog and at the bottom instead of striking out towards the distant sea they had turned left to go up the estuary. Round the curve of the cliff the woods came down to meet the sand and Aunt Fliss turned in under the trees. They came to a little gate in a wall nearly lost in undergrowth and she had unlocked an ancient rusting padlock. Bending down under overhanging branches they followed an almost indistinguishable path for a few moments and then, straightening up, Aunt Fliss had said, 'There you are. How about that?' And there it was in front of him. About five hundred yards in length the pool was oval in shape and they were standing on one of the long sides completely overhung with shrubs and trees. The sun high overhead struck brilliant shafts of light from the slow spreading ripples in the wake of a couple of moorhens chugging across. Moored a little further along the bank was a rowing boat. There wasn't a sound except for faint rustlings from the green gloom around them and the gentle slap of water at their feet. Simon had drawn a deep breath.

'It doesn't look as if anybody comes here.'

'Nobody does,' she had said. 'The children from the big house used to use it but no one comes now. It's private land you see, the holiday makers don't even know it's here, they only look towards the sea but we keep the gate locked just in case. The boat is mine, I used to fish a bit. There were trout in here, I don't know whether there are now, but you can come here whenever you like, swim, use the boat. It'll be your private place.'

He couldn't speak, his throat was so tight, but she didn't seem to expect an answer. Instead she stripped off the faded towelling robe she was wearing and slid into the water like an old brown otter. He followed and they swam and floated peacefully about until she said, 'Time for some breakfast I think,' and they went back through the little gate and up the cliff path, to thick bacon sandwiches and mugs of tea, sitting companionably together on the doorstep in the sunshine. She had hung the padlock key on a peg just inside the back door and said, 'Take it whenever you like but don't forget to lock up behind you.'

He had felt as if he had been given the best present of his whole life and didn't know how to thank her but it didn't seem to matter. It was as if she knew and that was enough.

He lay on his back now, floating, staring up at the unbelievably blue sky, remembering. Not just the seemingly endless summers of his teenage but the terrible winter after Aunt Fliss died. The miserable funeral in the biting cold of a bleak December afternoon at the little church on the headland, Hester not the sleek golden goddess he'd always known but thin and pinched, pale-faced and red-eyed. And then the letter waiting for him at his grandfather's house when he arrived home from university. ' I'm afraid Christmas is off this year, Simon,' she had written. 'I'm going down to the cottage to sort out Fliss's things. You would probably be better staying with your grandfather, there's not much point in coming to London unless you want to keep your father company, but I think he's already tied up.'

He had left for London by the next train to find Oliver in his usual haze of whisky, alternately cursing and sobbing that Hester was a bitch, a stupid heartless cow. Nobody understood what he was going through, all those bastards at the BBC had got their knives into him, and so on and so on, the same dreary litany that Simon had heard so many times before. He had stood over his father, so sick with furious disgust at the mumbling wreck in front of him that he wanted to choke, but he simply said, 'So she's gone to the cottage then,' turned on his heel and left.

By train to Plymouth and then a taxi for the last ten miles down to the cove. He had found her, sitting by the fire, piles of papers all around her, staring at a photograph of the three of them, he and she and Fliss, standing in front of the cottage squinting and laughing into the sun. As the latch had clicked she had looked up and held out a hand. He had gathered her up and rocked her while she cried and cried until there were no tears left. They had stayed there all through the Christmas holidays, packing, sorting and throwing out and cleaning the cottage from top to bottom. Neither of them mentioned Oliver, it seemed an unspoken agreement and he had not phoned. On Simon's last evening they went up to the pub for a meal and when they got back Hester got out a bottle of Fliss's elderberry wine and two beautiful etched glasses. They sat either side of the fire and Simon had watched her pour out the thick, almost black liquid. He held his glass to the light and the colour turned a deep purple.

'To Fliss,' he said quietly, 'thank you for the best times in my whole life.'

'To Fliss,' Hester echoed softly and they sipped the warm syrupy wine.

'I'm not going back, Simon,' she said abruptly, putting down her glass. 'Not ever.'

'May I ask why or don't you want to say?'

'Didn't Oliver say anything?'

'Only the same old rubbish. He was out of his tree as usual.'

'He didn't tell you that I came back from Fliss's funeral to find him humping the bar maid from the Kings Head in my bed?'

Simon sat staring at her, appalled.

'Oh for God's sake. He is totally disgusting. What did you do?'

Hester picked up her glass with a reminiscent smile.

'They were so—er... busy they didn't hear me come in. I got a pan of cold water and threw it all over them.'

Simon started to laugh. 'Hester, you didn't!'

She began to laugh too and then they were both shrieking, howling, laughing with tears running down their faces.

'I did, I did,' she was trying to control her voice, 'I was so bloody angry, not even upset just so bloody, bloody angry. I mean, it's what you do to cats and dogs if you want them to stop going at it.' She was wiping her eyes with the back of her hand before going off into another gale of laughter.

'There was her great, fat, white bottom bobbing up and down and when the water hit it she just collapsed on top of him. I should think she damaged him for life. I do hope so, I really do.'

She sobered suddenly and leant forward to put another log on the fire. Then she said slowly, 'I don't have to go back you see. We always thought Fliss lived here like she did, so simply, because she had no money, but we were wrong. She lived like that because she wanted to. Actually there's quite a lot of money and she's left it all to me.'

'Hester, that's wonderful. So are you going to live here all the time? What will you do with yourself?'

She smiled at him with such intensity he felt scorched.

'I'm going to realise my dream.'

'What is your dream?'

'I'm going to apply for planning permission to turn 'Coastguards' into a restaurant.'

He stared at her. 'You'll never get permission. Anyway, it's miles away from anywhere and it's not big enough.'

She continued to smile.

'Did you never wonder why no one had ever bought the cottage next door?'

'Well, it's almost derelict. It's been closed up for years.'

'It belonged to Fliss. She bought it when the old lady died and later the one next to it which she turned into the 'Gallery'. She didn't originally intend to use them, she just didn't want anyone else here. So I can extend into that.'

He had sat for a long time trying to come to terms with what she was telling him. No more lovely, lazy, sunlit holidays. It was the end of an era. But it was obvious that for her it was the exciting start of a new one. She was going to build on everything this place had meant to her to make a different, more satisfying life.

'And Dad?' he asked finally.

Her face closed. 'I realised, once I got here, after only a day or two, that it's been over for a long time. We've just been going through the motions. I'm sorry, Simon, but I'm not going to spend the rest of my life nannying a hopeless drunk. He's blown every chance he's ever had, with me, with everyone. It's time to move on.'

'Do you think he'll let you?'

'He doesn't have a choice. He's only been here once. Thank God it rained the whole time and he hated it. He's an urban animal. He's got the flat, I persuaded him to buy that when he was on a high. It's all paid for and worth ten times what he paid for it. Perhaps not having me there, paying the bills, will sort him out. Anyway, he's on his own now.'

'And me?'

She leant forward to touch him. 'Simon, you know you will be welcome always. There will be a room for you to come whenever you want.'

And so it had been. She had fought and fought for planning permission and finally won. Within two years the restaurant was up and running. A battle at first but gradually success had come. And now, he thought turning over and swimming toward the bank, he was going to take a hand. He would realise his dream and they would share it together.

'Well, Simon, what is this momentous life-changing decision you have made?'

Hester was facing him across the table in the dark little wine bar where they had chosen to have lunch. Her tone was definitely ironic and he felt an unaccustomed surge of irritation. It was more than time she stopped treating him like a child. Once he told her his plans she would see that things were going to be very different from now on. But his voice was perfectly calm and pleasant when he replied.

'You know that Grandfather left me everything.'

'Yes, I've no idea what 'everything' entails but I imagine that you no longer have any money worries.'

'You could say that. I've almost completed the sale of the house so combined with his shares and so on I think you could say I'm quite comfortable.'

He named a figure that made her eyes widen and she gave a startled gasp. 'Good Lord, I'd no idea he was so well off.'

'Well it's mostly the money from the house. I knew those crescent houses must be worth a fair bit but as they so rarely come on the market I had no real idea. Anyway I don't need to worry about teaching at that bloody college anymore. I knew roughly how I was fixed at Easter so I gave my notice in then. I've finished there for good.'

Hester leant back in her chair and eyed him warily. Something about this was making her feel uneasy. She took a sip of wine.

'So what are you going to do now?'

'Well—' He leant forward, elbows on the table, his eyes fixed on her face. She shifted in her chair. The intensity of his expression was somehow faintly alarming.

'Well, yes, what?' she said more sharply than she

intended.

'I should have thought you might have had some idea,' he said. He sounded more threatening than teasing and again she felt a frisson of alarm.

'Well, I haven't, so do get on with it, you're making me feel quite nervous.'

'No need to be nervous.' He was oddly smug. 'You're going to be happier than you can possibly imagine.'

'I'm already perfectly happy, Simon. I hope you are not going to offer me money because I should refuse. I'm managing very well as it is.' Why did she feel so panicked and why was she being so rude? She pulled herself up.

'I'm sorry. That sounded awful. I didn't mean to sound so rude. Tell me what you plan to do.'

'Live here. Where else?'

She stared at him. 'Here. How do you mean? In this town? In Devon? Where?'

'At 'Coastguards' of course. With you.'

Hester felt as if somebody had plunged her into icy water. She sat rigidly, unable to speak or move.

Simon leant over and poured some more wine into her glass.

'Don't look like that, Hester. I'm sorry if I've surprised you but you'll soon see. It's the perfect answer.'

She found her voice. 'Answer to what? You sound as if there has been a problem to which you have found the solution. I have'—she corrected herself—'had no problem but this sounds as if there might now be one.'

Simon leant back in his chair, gently tilting his glass from side to side watching the movement of the wine. His face was very serene now, faintly smiling, and again she felt the odd surge of alarm.

'Simon, you can't announce out of the blue that you're going to come and live with someone without asking them how they feel about it.' She stopped and waited but he said nothing, just continued swirling his wine and smiling.

21

Suddenly she wanted to scream very loudly and run out of the wine bar and away from him, away from this whole ludicrous idea that he was so calmly assuming was their future. She caught hold of herself and forced her voice down to a calm, reasonable level.

'Simon. I'm truly sorry if you felt that this was a foregone conclusion but it absolutely isn't. Why do you think I don't live with anyone, haven't done for fourteen years since I left your father?'

'Well, why would you? There's been no one you want to live with. There hasn't been anyone since Father.' He sounded so certain she wanted to slap him.

'You cannot really suppose I've been leading a totally celibate life. Of course, there have been people, friends, lovers. But I have never wanted to share my space with anyone and I still don't want to. I'm sorry, Simon, but it's simply not on.'

His face had gone tight and very still while she was speaking and she was aware of his fingers so tightly clenched around the stem of his glass that his knuckles were white. For a few moments he said nothing then his hand relaxed and he tilted the glass to swallow the last of his wine and smiled at her.

'Yes, well that's all over now. There's no need to talk about the past. It's the future that matters. I've thought it all out. Nobody uses the gallery anymore do they? It's got electricity and running water. It'll make a marvellous studio flat and all we need to do is knock a door through into your bit and there we are. We shan't get under each other's feet but we shall be together. It's perfect. I'll open it up when we get back and have a good look round. It shouldn't take long to sort out.'

He got up and put out a hand. 'Come on, let's get back. Now it's all settled I can't wait to get started.'

* * *

22

Knock a door through! Into your bit! We shall be together! It'll be perfect! Hester walked ahead of him into the sizzling sunshine feeling cold to the depths of her being. She could not remember ever feeling so trapped. The ground felt rubbery under her feet and when Simon cupped her elbow as they crossed the road she wanted to flinch away. Inwardly she shook herself. This is completely ridiculous. This is Simon for God's sake, not some imaginary monster. He just hasn't understood. Once he'd calmed down she would talk to him again, make him understand. The mere idea of living with anyone after all these years panicked her. It was only her long habit of affection and duty that had allowed him the run of the flat in his holidays. Driving home in silence beside him she began to rehearse what she would say.

As they drew up at the back of the house she saw a familiar battered blue pickup parked in the corner. Hell, she thought, the last thing I need at this moment is Frank. Where is he anyway? I locked up so he can't be in the house.

'Who's that?' asked Simon as they walked toward the back door.

'It's just Frank. He's probably brought me some crabs. He must be round the front somewhere.'

As they walked through the passage they heard Tessa laughing. Coming out onto the terrace they saw her sitting at one of the tables with a burly middle-aged man in jeans and denim shirt, a tray of tea between them. They were deep in conversation and didn't notice the other two until they reached the table. The fisherman rose to his feet.

'Hi, young Simon, how's it going then? Down for your hols?'

The deep voice with a strong Devon burr was faintly patronising and Simon shook the outstretched hand abruptly.

'That's right, only it's not just holidays now. I'll get the key, Hester, I noticed it's still on the nail. No time like the present, that gallery is going to need a bit of an airing before it's fit for habitation.' He turned away and went back into the house and Hester sat down heavily.

'Is that tea fresh? I need a cup.'

Tessa said, 'No, it's cold. I'll go and make some more.' She picked up the tray and disappeared into the caravan.

Frank sat down opposite Hester, frowning slightly.

'What's he on about? Not just the holidays—what's going on?'

He stretched his hand out to touch hers and she drew it sharply away.

'Do be careful, he might see, so might Tess. We don't need speculation, particularly at the moment.'

His frown deepened. 'Why particularly now?'

She gave a huge sigh. 'I don't know how to deal with this and I really don't know how it's got to this point but Simon has decided he's coming to live with me and I can't seem to make him understand that he's not.'

'You must be joking.' Frank was incredulous. 'Stupid bugger. How old is he—thirty-four or five? He wants to come home and live with Mummy, does he? Tell him to get on his bike.'

'I've tried. He just won't seem to take it in. He's made his mind up, he doesn't hear anything I say.'

'Well you'll have to make him listen. Apart from anything else, where does that leave us?'

'Exactly,' she said helplessly and they sat silently staring at each other. After a few moments she asked, 'How's Alice?'

He shifted his gaze out to sea. 'Back in hospital. She's really bad this time. I had a good chat to the doctor. He doesn't think it can be much longer.'

'Poor Alice.' Her voice was very quiet. 'She suffers so much one can't wish for it to go on.'

He rubbed his hand over his face in a weary gesture.

'I don't. For her sake, or mine. Or her mother's. But you can't wish your wife dead, even when you know it'd be the best thing all round.'

She watched his averted face. Five years, give or take, they had been lovers. A mutually satisfactory agreement. He was a good lover, warm, tactile, considerate and fun in bed. She had never really felt guilty about Alice. Married at twenty, unable to have the children they both desperately wanted. By thirty diagnosed with multiple sclerosis, slight symptoms at first but worsening rapidly and leaving her completely bed ridden for the last three years. Devotedly nursed by her elderly mother and Frank between them. Frank and Hester saw little of each other during the summer season, both busy with the influx of visitors, he on his boat, she in the restaurant. An occasional snatched day with a picnic was about all they could manage. Both were completely agreed on secrecy. Alice must never find out and be upset. But in the winter they had far more time together. Lazy evenings by the fire, days, even the odd night away. It suited them perfectly. Even the enforced discretion added spice and kept the relationship going at a sexual pitch that would probably have subsided and faded away under other circumstances. Most important to Hester, her precious space was not invaded in any permanent way and she was still completely free and independent. But for how much longer?

Frank became aware of her watching him and turned back to face her.

'So what are you going to do, girl? He can't stay here. Someone's got to tell him. It's time he grew up. Do you want me to have a word?'

She gave a short laugh. 'Oh he's going to take it from you, isn't he? He's always been funny with you, it's almost as if he senses something.'

Frank frowned. 'So what's his problem? He can't mind about me on his father's account. He hates him even

25

though he does live with him. I've always thought that was a weird situation, I mean why didn't he cut loose years ago?'

She sighed. 'I've always supposed it was economic as much as anything. London's expensive, living with Oliver suited him financially and they pretty much led their own lives. But now—I don't know anymore. Perhaps he can't function on his own and now he doesn't need to work anymore he can choose where he lives and he's chosen here.'

'Well he can unchoose,' Frank snapped. 'It's plain ridiculous. You've got your own life to lead. He'll smother you. It's not on.'

'I know, I know,' she said tiredly. 'I've got to make him see. I'll have another go tomorrow.'

Frank rose to his feet. 'You coming down the pub tonight?'

'Probably, I'll see if Tessa wants to come.'

'And his lordship no doubt.'

'I expect so. I can hardly leave him behind.'

'Oh no. No one to tuck him in and read him a bed time story.'

Heavily sarcastic, Frank was more perturbed than he cared to show but it was time for visiting at the hospital.

'I'll be off then, see you later perhaps.' And he was gone. She heard the old diesel start up and fade into the distance and she suddenly felt very alone.

'Tea,' said Tessa's voice and she set the tray down. 'I waited. It looked as if you two were having a very serious discussion. I thought it best not to interrupt.'

'Thank you, Tess, that was tactful. I do have a pretty serious problem and Frank is a very old friend. I thought it might help to talk about it.'

'And did it?' Tessa asked pouring the tea.

'Not a lot, but I don't think anybody can solve this except me.'

'Right.' Tessa passed a cup over and sat down opposite her. There was silence for a few minutes and then Tessa said, tentatively, 'I don't want to be nosy but if you want to talk I'm here.'

Hester smiled at her. The big brown eyes under the glossy black fringe were kind and concerned. What a thoroughly nice person she was, Hester thought, so genuine and straightforward. For a moment she felt tempted but she shook her head.

'Thanks, Tess. I might take you up on that later but I've got to try and sort it out myself first.'

Simon came across the grass and sat down.

'I've opened all the windows,' he said cheerfully. 'The spiders weren't happy, scuttling about all over the place. It needs completely doing up. I'll go into town tomorrow and get some shade cards. I didn't realise there was a little kitchen there already. At least, a sink and a Baby Belling. It'll be easy to plumb a shower in next to it and fit it all out properly. It's going to be great.'

He got up, smiling down at them both. 'I'm for a swim, anyone coming?'

Hester rose slowly. 'I don't think so. I'll go in and have a nice leisurely bath. See you both later. I'm going to the pub about nine. Do you fancy coming, Tess?' She shot an entreating look at Tessa.

'Sure, why not?' Tessa responded comfortably not looking at Simon. She picked up the tray and ambled off to the caravan but as soon as she was inside she turned to the window and watched the pair walking stiffly across the lawn. That, she said to herself, is very bad body language. I have the strongest feeling that something is seriously wrong.

Chapter 3

They were sitting with their coffee the following morning after completing the week's menus when Tessa said casually, 'Is Simon coming to live here permanently?'

'What has he said to you exactly?' Hester said abruptly. 'I saw you talking for ages last night in the pub.'

Tessa poured the last of the coffee into their mugs and sat back.

'Well, according to him it's always been understood that one day you'd live together.'

'In his dreams.' Hester's voice rose. 'I don't understand where he's got this idea from. It's never even been mentioned between us, it's all in his head.'

Tessa asked 'What is this 'gallery' he keeps talking about?'

'You'll have noticed the empty bit at the far end beyond the restaurant. There was once a third cottage, which hasn't been lived in for years. Fliss bought it when she bought next door. She needed to make it safe but the upper floor was very dodgy so it was gutted and made into one huge room with the staircase leading to a mezzanine. She rented it out to some local artists and craftsmen to show their work. She was a gifted painter herself. The abstracts in the sitting room are hers. The gallery was quite well known for some years but gradually the others gave up or died off and it was closed up. I have been asked to open it for weddings and so on but it would need a good bit doing to bring it up to scratch and I'm not keen so it's just been left. I never wanted the restaurant to get beyond what I could manage by myself with the help I've got. Now Simon thinks he's going to turn it into a studio flat.' She looked helplessly at Tessa. 'Do you think I'm being mean and unreasonable? Is that how it looks to an outsider?'

'No,' said Tessa decidedly. 'If you wanted to have

anyone here you could have rented it out ages ago. It's not as if he's on his uppers with no money and nowhere to go. If he wants to live round here he can buy something, there's loads of property for sale along this coast.' She hesitated and then went on, 'It's none of my business and I've only just met him but has he always been so obsessive about you and this place?'

Hester stared out of the window at the gleaming sea.

'I know, it's always been special to him. I understand that, it is to me. I've been coming here since I was a child. My parents never took me on holiday. They used to dump me with Fliss while they went abroad but I didn't mind. I loved it. They were so boring and stuffy and dull and she was amazing. Unique. I had more fun...' Her voice trailed away, her eyes still turned toward the bay. She sighed.

'I wanted Simon to have what I'd had. Poor little boy. He'd lived such a miserable life stuck in that grim house with those old people.'

'I don't want to intrude, but how did you meet his father?'

'He was in the Repertory Theatre for the summer season and I went with a friend. He was the lead, incredibly handsome then. I fell totally in love that first night. We went round to the pub next door after the performance and they were all there. My friend went up and asked for his autograph and that was it. They bought us drinks and we used to go nearly every evening after that. I was completely hooked.'

'And when the season ended?'

'He asked me to go and live with him in London and I did. Without a backward glance. My parents were absolutely stunned, they wouldn't even meet him. He was still married to someone else but he hadn't lived with her for a couple of years, just hadn't bothered to divorce.'

'And you never got married?'

'No. At first it didn't matter and later I didn't want to.

I've never wanted children. Having Simon in the holidays was enough and anyway it soon became obvious I was going to have to work to keep us both going when Oliver was 'resting'. That's when I started cooking professionally.'

Tessa said carefully, 'Am I right in thinking that Oliver was pretty well known at one time wasn't he?'

'Oh yes. He had some good West End runs and a couple of television series. At first he only drank seriously when he wasn't working. He could always control it when he'd got something going on, but gradually it took over. There were some really bad incidents and he became completely unreliable so of course the work dried up. They didn't renew his contract and that was that. I'd basically been keeping him for about three years when Fliss died.'

She smiled suddenly at Tessa. 'Why on earth am I telling you all this? You must be bored to tears.'

'Absolutely not,' Tessa grinned. 'I'd love you to go on but I can't help thinking that it doesn't help your present problem does it.'

'No,' Hester replied gloomily. 'I'm going to have to make him understand but it's very difficult because one part of me sympathises with him. But it won't work. He wants too much of me, we won't really be living separately whatever he says. He'd be round my neck the whole time, I can feel it. The only reason it's been OK up to now is because he's always had to go back.'

'If you don't mind my asking, what exactly is the age difference between you if it's not too rude a question?'

'Eleven years. Why?'

'Nothing really.' Tessa started to gather up the coffee mugs and menus. 'Time we got started.' She paused, looking down at Hester. 'I don't know what to say to you about this except that I think you're absolutely right to resist and you should keep on until he gets the message.'

Her gaze shifted to the doorway. A girl was standing there, silently watching them. Hester followed her glance and stood up.

'I'm sorry,' she said. 'Were you wanting coffee? I'm afraid we're only open in the evenings.'

'I don't want coffee,' the girl said in a high drawling voice, 'I've come to see Simon Brown. Do you know where he is?'

There was a small silence while Hester and Tessa both stared at her. She gazed back enquiringly and asked again, 'Is he here?'

Hester pulled herself together. 'Not at the moment I'm afraid. He's gone into town. He should be back by lunchtime.'

'I'll wait,' she said and went outside. They watched her walk across the lawn and sit down at one of the tables. She was small and thin and very pretty with long reddish hair and pale clear skin, slightly freckled. She slung her rucksack onto the table and taking a book out calmly settled down to read.

Tessa drew a deep breath. 'She's pretty cool. Who is she?'

'I haven't the faintest idea,' Hester replied still watching the girl, 'but whoever she is I have the feeling Simon is not going to be pleased she's here.'

He was not. He came, whistling, into the kitchen, a sheaf of colour charts in his hand.

'Hi, everybody, any chance of lunch?'

Molly and Joan, reliable, sensible and grey-haired who came every day from the village to help, gazed adoringly at him and offered in unison to get him something to eat.

'You certainly won't,' Hester snapped. 'If he wants anything he can get it himself. You've quite enough to do. And you'd better take your friend something, Simon, she's been waiting long enough.'

'What friend?' he asked, puzzled.

'That one out there.' Hester nodded toward the garden.

He walked over to the window and stared out. When

31

he turned back his face was expressionless.

'She's not a friend and she's no business here,' he said tightly. 'I'll sort it.' They watched him walk across the grass and the girl rose to meet him. Tessa met Hester's eyes.

'Phew. I think he's angry, really really angry.'

'Wasn't he just. Quite scary. Let's wait and see.'

In between preparing the evening's meal they glanced out of the window and it was quite apparent that a furious argument had developed. Eventually the raised voices reached such a pitch that they could catch some of what was being said.

Simon's voice, raw and cruel:

'Doesn't it occur to you that if I wanted you to come here I'd have asked you? I told you a month ago, it's over, finished. How dare you follow me here, and how the hell did you find out where I was?'

'I asked your father.' The girl sounded breathless, stumbling a little over her words as if amazed at the fury she had unleashed.

'You-asked-my-father.' Each word was bitten off in cold disbelief. 'You have been to the flat? How did you get the address?'

'I-I followed you home one night.' She was gathering some defiance. 'You would never ask me to your house. I just wanted to see where you lived. I couldn't see why you never asked me.'

'Well now you've met my father perhaps you understand rather better. I would have preferred the college not to know my parent is a hopeless dribbling alcoholic.'

'Simon, I'm sorry.' She stretched out a hand but he stepped sharply back and the hand dropped. 'I wouldn't dream of telling anyone, of course I wouldn't.'

He stared at her coldly. 'It doesn't really matter, I shan't be seeing any of them again.'

'What do you mean?' Her voice was wavering now.

'I finished with the college, I'm not going back.'

'You mean you've left? Without telling me?'

'Why should I tell you? I have already said, whatever we had was finished. Done with. I thought I'd made that perfectly clear.'

'Simon, please.' They could hear her tears now. 'What have I done? You can't mean this. Please tell me what I've done.'

He stepped back a further pace as if to distance himself as much as possible.

'Nothing. You have done nothing. You've just been building castles with no foundation. I thought you understood. It was nice while it lasted but it never meant anything. I thought you realised that.'

'It didn't mean anything?' She sounded dazed. 'Simon, I love you. How can you say this?'

'Did I ever say I loved you?' His voice had been cold before but now it was icy.

'Well no, but I knew you did. You must have done.'

'You stupid, stupid little cow.' He was shouting now. 'Love, love, you don't have a clue. Go home and play with your dolls and don't ever come here again.'

He turned away from her, stood indecisively for a moment and then made for the cliff path and disappeared. She stood looking after him for a moment and then dropped onto the grass, her face in her hands.

Hester drew a deep breath.

'Take her some hot coffee, Tess, and see if you can't sort her out. I don't think I had better get involved. It sounds as if he's been a complete bastard but we don't know both sides.'

She watched Tessa go over to the girl and touch her shoulder. She helped her up and sat her at the table, persuading her to drink the coffee, talking quietly and persuasively. Gradually the convulsive sobs died away. She scrubbed at her face with a crumpled wedge of tissue and began to respond to what Tessa was saying. They sat together for some time talking earnestly and finally got up and walked away around the house. Hester heard a car drive off and Tessa came back into the kitchen. Hester glanced towards Molly and Joan who were studiously pretending a complete lack of interest and shook her head slightly. Tessa nodded and went over to the cooker and began frying off meat. Hester started talking to the women about the coming evening and gradually the atmosphere eased.

It wasn't until early afternoon when Joan and Molly had driven off in their ancient Mini, that Hester and Tessa sat down to a late lunch of crab sandwiches and a jug of fresh lemonade in the shade of the willow.

Biting into the crusty bread Hester said, 'He's not come back yet. He must be walking it off.'

Tessa said seriously, 'You know he's really beginning to worry me. Do you know want to know what she said?'

'Of course I want to know. I'm burning with curiosity.'

Tessa took a long swallow of her drink. 'As you said, one would need to hear both sides and, to be fair, he didn't promise her anything, but it's the pattern that's so weird.'

'The pattern?'

'Yes. From what she said he does this every year. He's notorious for it but clever. He never chooses the straight-from-school students, they're always third-years.'

'What do you mean?'

'Well. That means they won't be back next year. He never picks one of his own students so there's no problem from the authority's point of view.'

'What do you mean, he picks them?'

'Apparently this has been a pattern over the last few years. He will start an affair with someone during the autumn term and finish it before the summer term ends. He never goes out with them socially, won't go to any occasions as a couple, and he never invites them home.'

'Well that I can understand, with Oliver there.'

'Yes,' Tessa said thoughtfully, 'but don't you think that may be one of the reasons it suits him to live with Oliver. It helps him to stay uninvolved. No question of anyone trying to move in. Of course with the girls it starts off almost as a game. Each one thinks I'll be the one to get him, that sort of thing, that's quite obviously what this one thought. But it's a dangerous game with someone like him.'

'What do you mean exactly?' Hester asked.

'He's just using them to suit himself. No one can reach him and they end up either disillusioned or heartbroken.'

'But why?' Hester was becoming exasperated. 'Why is he like this? Do you think it all stems back to his childhood? Can't love because he wasn't loved? That kind of psychological stuff?'

Tessa seemed to be trying to choose her words. 'Possibly. I don't know anything about psychology but there is obviously a problem. I think it may be more complex than that.'

'What sort of complex?'

Tessa hesitated. 'Really, I don't know. Anyway, I'm afraid she's not just giving up. She's staying with friends in Plymouth and she says she's coming back.'

Hester was aghast. 'Oh no. Do we tell Simon?'

'I certainly wouldn't,' Tessa said firmly. 'We stay well out of it and make for the bomb shelter if necessary.'

Hester laughed rather shakily. 'I can't believe life seemed so simple two days ago, but you're right, we will stand well back and wait and see.'

Tessa stretched. 'OK. Well, I'm going for a swim.' She started towards the caravan and then stopped and turned back. 'There's one more thing. He always chooses redheads. One of his girlfriends was a natural blonde but she had dyed her hair red. When he realised he dropped her flat. She was furious and told everybody.'

Hester said thoughtfully, 'Now that's weird. Why this hang up with red hair?'

Tessa's eyes rested on her employer's thick chestnut mane but she said nothing except, 'See you later,' and went into the caravan.

Chapter 4

Simon did not appear again until just before dinner and then he breezed into the kitchen as if nothing had happened.

'Do you need any help tonight, Hester?' he asked. 'I'll do the bar or wait table, whatever.'

She looked up at him, searchingly, but his expression was as unruffled as his manner.

'I don't think so, Simon, unless we get some extras who haven't booked. You can have a quiet evening in the flat.'

'OK. I'll go and have a shower. I might come down later and see who's about.'

It was on the tip of Hester's tongue to tell him to do as he was told. She didn't want him hanging around the restaurant ingratiating himself with her customers, making himself part of the local scene but she realised she was being foolish. He was already known and accepted, he'd been coming down on holiday for so long and he was well liked. He was good-looking, charming and single, enough to recommend him to all the women, and the men seemed happy to tolerate him. So she said nothing.

Later, watching him sitting at the bar, laughing and joking with a group of elderly regulars, something struck her that she had never thought about before. He always spent time with older people, he never chatted to younger ones or attempted to join in a group of his contemporaries. Perhaps he was still basically shy and felt more comfortable with people of the age group with whom he had spent so much time as a child. She was almost beginning to feel the old familiar concern and protectiveness when one of the group patted her arm as they were leaving, saying, 'How lovely for you, Hester dear. Simon tells us he's coming to live down here permanently. That'll be such a help for you, and company too.'

Immediately fury and panic rose in her. How dare he do this! Trying to trap her into accepting his idiotic plans. Seething with anger and frustration she stomped into the kitchen to see Tessa replacing the handset on the wall phone. Her cheeks were flushed and she was wearing an expression Hester had not seen before. Excited and glowing.

'Well, you look happy enough,' she said sharply. 'I'm glad someone is. What's going on?'

'Well—it's Tim, my fiancé. He's got a few days off and he's coming down. I wondered—er—no, it doesn't matter.'

'Well, what? What is it? You might as well say.' Hester knew she was being tetchy and unreasonable but somehow she couldn't stop herself. 'Well, come on, Tessa, out with it.'

'I just wondered if you would allow him to stay with me in the caravan. It's only for three nights but it's probably a bad idea. Forget it. I'm sorry I asked.' She turned away back to the sink.

There was total silence for a minute and Hester said quietly, 'Of course he can stay, as long as he realises that you've still got to work. I didn't even know you'd got a fiancé. You kept that very quiet.'

Tessa turned to face her with a nervous smile. 'Well you made it clear at the beginning that you weren't interested in private lives and that was fine by me. I've come here to work and my life at home has nothing to do with this but Tim's father has taken on a student to do two months work experience with him so it's given Tim a chance for a few days off.'

'What do you mean exactly? What does Tim do?'

'He's a vet, he qualified this year and he's started in practice with his father, the other partner has just retired and Tim's taken over.'

Listening to her talking of her fiancé with this special

note in her voice and soft expression in her eyes, Hester felt somehow confused and ashamed. What sort of selfish, self-absorbed person was she that Tessa had been working closely with her for almost three months and she hadn't even known the girl was engaged to be married. So deeply involved in her own tight little world that she had no interest in anything outside it. No wonder she felt so terrified of the invasion that Simon seemed about to make on it.

'Of course he can come,' she replied warmly. 'When will he be here?'

'Not 'til Saturday and he'll go back on Tuesday, then we can have Monday together. Is that really OK?'

'Of course. Ring him and tell him he can come.' She hesitated. 'I'm sorry, Tess, I didn't mean to be so bitchy. It was just...' She stopped abruptly.

'Simon?' Tessa enquired.

Hester sighed. 'Yes. Simon. He's really got me spooked.'

'Do you want to talk about it?'

Hester sighed again. 'Not now,' she said wearily, 'tomorrow perhaps when my mind is clearer.' She looked round the quiet tidy kitchen.

'You are good, you've done it all. Thanks. I think I'll be off to bed. Goodnight.'

* * *

Tessa looked after her. Poor bloody woman, she thought. She'd got her world so beautifully arranged and this weirdo is pulling it down round her ears. And that is what he is, she said to herself as she switched off the light and locked the door. Weird and somehow scary and Hester doesn't seem to realise it. I suppose you don't when it's family and you're that close to it. But he certainly worries me.

The weather broke the next night. The day had been breathless with heat and toward early evening huge clouds had started to mass on the horizon and the sky turned copper-coloured. The restaurant had been packed and people seemed reluctant to leave, spilling out onto the grass when their meals were finished, taking their wine with them, chattering and gazing at the spectacular view. The strange fading light had given the cove the aspect of a stage set, beautiful but vaguely sinister and the guests were obviously enjoying the atmosphere.

Hester had finally fallen into bed exhausted, to be jerked awake by a deafening crash of thunder. Jagged streaks of lightning lit the room and repeated crashes and rumbles decided her against attempting further sleep. She switched on the bedside lamp to try to reduce the effect of the lightning and got up to shut the window and close the curtains. For a moment she stood at the window staring out. The wind had risen and rain was beginning to spatter angrily on the glass. She shivered suddenly, dragged the curtain tight, and scrambled back into bed. Pulling the duvet up she plumped up the pillows behind her and leant back, her mind moving directly towards the ever-present problem. Simon.

What was she going to do? She suddenly wished urgently for someone to talk to, someone who knew her well, knew Simon and his history, who would understand but see it all objectively. Someone who could advise her but was not involved. No good talking to Frank. He was definitely biased. Tess too had made her views very clear, besides she was too near to the situation. It suddenly occurred to Hester that she had no close woman friend to hand. Her friends were scattered around the country, people she would see on a round of visits during her winter break, to relax and have fun with, but no one she could phone at a moment's notice and dump her problems on. Since Fliss had died she had never felt the need for a confidante. Her father was dead, her mother a Bridge playing gossip in an expensive retirement home visited three or four times a year from courtesy only. There really was no one she felt could enter into her feelings over this except—with a rush of warmth she thought of Peter—he was just the person but where was he? What far flung corner of the globe was he observing and commenting on, how would she reach him? The warmth drained away as quickly as it had come. There was no instant access to Peter and never had been. That was the problem. She still remembered their first meeting.

It was during the preliminary stages of her first television series. A producer who was spending a holiday in the area and been brought to the restaurant by friends had approached her. He had immediately recognised the potential for a successful cookery format with this charismatic woman who had made such a stunning success of such a crazy venture. After much discussion and several visits to London it had been decided to film a series of six programmes during the closed period for the restaurant starting at New Year.

On her first morning she had gone to the canteen for coffee and stood in the queue next to a very tall, thin man in a rumpled suit with a shock of unruly grey hair. It wasn't until he turned his profile towards her that she recognised him. Peter Armitage, television journalist, famous for his coverage of trouble. Trouble of every kind in every place —war, famine, plague, disaster—he was there. His deeply lined face was familiar in millions of living rooms worldwide as he described unbelievable horrors in a quiet, everyday voice which was so much more compelling than the excited staccato delivery used by many commentators. She was so startled to find him beside her that she fumbled getting her purse out of her bag and upset her cup of coffee. To her horror she realised that she had splashed the back of his jacket. For a moment she cravenly thought of saying nothing but almost before this thought was formed she heard herself saying, 'Excuse me, I'm terribly sorry but…' And that had been the start of it.

Completely unconcerned about his jacket he had smiled at her with a warmth she had never seen on the screen.

'You're new aren't you, or is it that I haven't been around for a while?'

Balancing his tray he had glanced around the packed canteen and spotted a table in the corner.

'Shall we?' he had questioned and without waiting for her to answer started purposefully across the room with Hester trotting obediently behind him.

The next three weeks had been a roller coaster. Snatched coffees, hurried lunches and longer leisurely evenings tucked away in small restaurants and pubs, talking, talking, talking. She was aware of the curiosity of his and her colleagues but neither of them offered explanation or responded to veiled questions. Hester was riding a wave of excitement with the series, which was going extremely well and with this challenging, fascinating, complex man who seemed to want to spend his every leisure minute with her. She did not examine what was happening, just fell into bed every night exhausted and rose again next day fizzing with energy and adrenaline, never before feeling so sizzlingly alive.

The blow fell without warning. They had settled into a table in one of their favourite haunts, a bistro wine bar not frequented by the television crowd. Peter poured them each a glass of wine and sat back, his hand loosely round the stem of his glass, frowning slightly at the contents. She waited quietly for him to speak, thinking him just tired after a long busy day, when he raised his head and looked across at her. Something in his face made her tense up, her stomach muscles contracting. He said, very quietly, 'I'm off again tomorrow, first thing.'

She went icy with shock. For a minute she couldn't speak and then in a voice so thin she hardly recognised it as her own she said, 'Why didn't you tell me before?'

He stared back into his glass. 'I didn't know. I rarely do. I go where and when I'm sent, you know that.'

She said nothing and he looked up. The misery she felt must have been written large on her face. He stretched out a hand and covered hers. For a long moment there was silence then he said, 'Did you not wonder why I haven't tried to sleep with you?'

'I thought…' Her voice failed and she tried again. 'I thought we had time. I thought that it would come. It felt inevitable—I believed—I really —' her voice failed again and she stared down at the table cloth which wavered and blurred.

'Hester, look at me.' The quiet voice was insistent and eventually she raised her eyes to his face. It was very still and intent, his eyes fixed on hers.

'I have been married twice, you know that, but we haven't discussed why I am not still married. I have accepted that it is mainly down to me. My job is the most important thing in my life and no woman can put up with it. That, and the constant absences, the fact that I cannot make any firm plans for holidays, for any social activity, for anything, has wrecked all my relationships. I have never really wanted children and a family life and that is not fair. The trouble was, the first time I married I didn't realise my priorities and the second time my wife believed she could cope with them, but she couldn't and I can't really blame her for that.'

His grip tightened on her hand. 'Look, as a permanent partner I'm a dead loss. And there's another thing. Doing what I do the dangers are very real. I know you can get knocked down crossing the road and I know the statistics for being in a car crash but my chances of sudden death are pretty high and I do not want the responsibility of someone at home worrying about me. I have to be, I must be, baggage free, as it were. So you see...'

He stopped. Hester continued to watch his face, saying nothing, and he stared back at her, waiting.

Eventually, she said, 'You must have realised what was happening to us, or have I got it all wrong? Have I imagined what I thought you felt?'

He dropped his gaze to their linked hands and slowly lifted her hand and held it against his face for a moment, kissed the palm and put it gently back on the table.

'No, you didn't imagine anything. When I met you that first morning I thought, what a gorgeous woman, this could be fun. That was all I intended, just fun. I certainly thought we would sleep together. It would be a pleasant interlude for both of us. No harm done. But within a couple of days it was different. What I should have done was knock it on the head then, but I didn't. Seeing you, being with you was such a huge pleasure I couldn't bring myself to deny it. We'll just be good friends, I thought, no complications.'

'And are we?'

He said soberly, 'Indeed I believe we are.'

'Is that all?'

He was silent for a moment and then said harshly, 'Of course it's bloody not. But I will not take it further. I may have fallen in love with you, Hester, but there is no life for us together and you have to accept that. I'm trying to behave decently, for God's sake. I know if we take that one more step we're lost. I shall be worrying about you, worrying about me, worrying about what you are doing, who you are seeing. I can't afford to and neither can you. I'm trying to be honest. I don't want the responsibilities of another human being and seeing what I see in my work makes ordinary human happiness seem pretty irrelevant. I'm sorry if that sounds harsh but it's true.'

44

He drained his glass and, glancing at her untouched wine, poured himself another one. There was a long silence, then Hester said softly, 'Will I see you when you come back? Just as your friend?'

He raised his eyes and looked at her. 'I want that more than anything if you are willing to put up with it. It will only be as and when, you do realise that?'

'Yes, I do. I would rather be your friend than nothing at all.'

It was several hours later that they finally left the little restaurant and walked back through a fine drizzle to Hester's hotel. Just before they reached it Peter had stopped under a lamp and tipped her chin up. He said, very quietly, 'It's no good. I cannot go away without at least knowing what it's like to kiss you.'

Hester lay in bed listening to the rattle of the rain on the window and felt her deep inner muscles contract at the memory. It had been like no other kiss she had given or received before or since. A searching, gentle, passionate giving and receiving of the strongest feeling she had ever known. It lasted a long time but she had been completely lost and unaware. When it had ended he had held her so hard and so close she felt she had melted, become disembodied, more part of him than she had ever been with anyone, even during the sexual act. When he left her outside the hotel he did not kiss her, simply said, 'I'll be in touch,' and was gone.

The wonderful warm certainty lasted until she woke the next day, to a chill grey London morning, and room service knocking at the door with an exquisite bouquet of forced spring flowers. The card read, 'To my dearest friend, I will be in touch. P.'

And then she wept for a long time, tearing desperate sobs of loss, desolation and frustration. Then she showered, dressed, did her face and went to the studio and no one said a word.

He had been in touch. Over the past six years, scribbled notes, post cards, occasional telephone calls or e-mails and every winter at some time during her New Year break he managed to be in London for a hasty few days and they would meet, to talk and walk and eat together. It was always an extraordinary, enchanted interlude. They never mixed with other people, it would have been a waste of time. They spent every waking moment of their few days together but never the nights, and Hester would lie in her hotel room, aching with a fierce desperate hunger but saying nothing the next day. She knew it must be like this or not at all and it was only bearable because she also knew with certainty that she was loved.

And this, she thought drearily, turning her pillows again to try and get comfortable, is exactly what he meant. When I really need him he cannot be here, or even contactable and I have to accept that and manage on my own. Frank was a sort of comfort blanket, a defence against total solitude, and a sexual release. Lying there, listening to the rain, she realised, as she had never done before, that this was all it was and that was why it worked. They both had their personal priorities, the only difference being that she knew about and accepted his, but he had no knowledge of her inner life at all. She smiled involuntarily. Frank didn't go in for inner life. What you saw was what you got and that was fine.

She must have dozed off because when she woke up a grey light was struggling through the curtains and the rain had stopped.

Chapter 5

But not for long. It rained fairly constantly for the next week, the fine insistent mizzle so peculiar to the West Country. The beach was deserted apart from some hardy souls in cagoules and walking boots rambling up the estuary but business was brisk. If they couldn't picnic on the beach, having dinner while gazing out seemed the next best thing. The restaurant was full every evening and Hester was too busy in the day and too tired at night to give serious thought to her problem. Simon spent most of the days either out or in the gallery and the evenings helping behind the bar or sitting at it chatting to customers. He was perfectly pleasant to Hester, but guarded, and she was just relieved that nothing else had been said for the moment. However, it proved to be the calm before the storm.

On Friday evening Tessa said, very quietly, as she passed Hester in the kitchen,

'She's back.'

For a moment Hester couldn't think what she meant and then it dawned.

'Simon's girl?'

'Yes. I've just seen her crossing the terrace with a couple of other people.'

'They must be the friends she's staying with. Oh Lord, I've got a feeling this could be nasty. Simon's behind the bar tonight so he can't walk away this time.' Peering through the glass panel in the service door, Hester could see the girl standing at the far end of the bar in conversation with a middle-aged couple. Simon was busy at the other end serving drinks but she could tell by his rigid expression that he knew the girl was there. As she watched he went up the bar to serve them and it was obvious that he was behaving as if they were all complete strangers. The male companion paid for the drinks and as

47

they were turning away the girl leant forward and said something to Simon. He stared at her blankly and at that moment the waitress came up and spoke to them, obviously suggesting they take their drinks to their waiting table. The girl went reluctantly, turning her head to look at Simon but he totally ignored her and started busying himself with some new customers.

This is ridiculous, thought Hester exasperatedly as she went back to the cooker, he can't simply pretend she's not there. He's going to have to deal with it.

When she went out later in her freshly pressed and gleaming whites the party was still there. From the girl's miserable face and the baleful looks being cast at Simon by the other two it was obvious they knew what was going on and heartily disapproved. As well they might, Hester thought wearily. I do hope there isn't going to be a public fuss. She went to her usual stool at the end of the bar where she would sit and chat to the departing guests and said to Simon, 'My usual, please.'

As he placed the long glass of lime and soda in front of her she said quietly, 'I hope you are going to deal with this business discreetly, Simon. I do not want a scene, so at least you had better speak to her.'

'I'll sort it,' he answered sharply and moved away.

A few minutes later the party rose to leave and the couple went to wait by the door while the girl came again to the bar and stood watching Simon. He left the people he was talking to and came over to her. Before she could speak he said curtly, 'Come over on Monday morning, we'll talk then.'

'Simon, please,' she said pleadingly, 'can't we..?'

He cut in, his voice low but the fury vibrating, 'For God's sake, Jennifer, don't make a scene. I said Monday. Now please go.' She lingered for a few moments more but he turned his back on her and went to the other end of the bar and, finally, she left, her woman friend casting a last venomous glance at Simon as they went out.

Hester drew a deep breath. This really was not what she wanted in her restaurant. Several of the regulars were looking curious, aware that some drama was going on and she did not want to start parrying questions. Fortunately everyone was on the point of leaving so apart from thanking her for the evening and a little light banter nothing further was said. When everyone had gone and the staff were tidying up Hester said, 'Simon, I'd like a word. Come up to the flat.'

He looked wary and mulish but he followed her up the stairs and when they reached the sitting room walked over to the window and stood with his back to her, hands in his pockets staring out. Hester sat down on the sofa and for a few moments there was silence. Eventually she said, 'Well, what do you propose to do about this business?'

'Get rid of her,' he replied tersely.

'Obviously this is nothing to do with me but aren't you perhaps being rather harsh?'

He flung round and stared down at her and unconsciously she flinched back. His anger was like an electric charge and she had never before seen such an expression on his face.

'Too bloody right it's not your business. You know nothing about it. The affair such as it was, was over weeks ago. She just won't accept it. Well she'll have to. I can't stand the sight of her. I want her out of here, she should never have come. If it wasn't for my stupid drunken father she would never have found me.'

He turned back abruptly to the window. Hester, shocked and shaken by his anger, stayed silent and after a moment he said very softly, 'This is our place. We don't need anybody else. I don't want to share it with anyone.'

Attempting to diffuse the taut atmosphere Hester said lightly, 'What about my customers. I don't think they'd be very happy, do you?'

He turned quickly, a completely different expression on his face, intent and eager.

'That's the point. You don't need customers, you don't need to work. I've got enough money for both of us. You could close the restaurant and we'd be free. Free to travel, to do whatever we like.'

She stared at him, bereft of speech. He crossed the space between them in a couple of strides and sat down beside her imprisoning both her hands between his.

'Think, Hester, think how marvellous it would be, we could go anywhere and there'd always be this place to come back to, just waiting for us. Our home, our own private paradise.'

She was rigid with shock, unable to speak or move. Then she dragged her hands away and stood up, her voice shaking.

'I think you've gone completely mad. Whatever are you thinking of? This is my life, the restaurant is my life. I love it. I'll never give it up. But you're right about one thing. This place is not for sharing, not with you, not with anyone. I will not have you living in the gallery trying to control me, trying to run my life. You must find your own place. I don't want you here. I'm sorry.' And she turned and fled to her bedroom shutting the door and leaning on it, her knees weak, as if they were about to give way.

Eventually she went over to the bed and sat down feeling as if she had been caught in a storm, battered and buffeted by elemental forces beyond her control. She strained to hear some sound that would tell her either that Simon was still there, waiting for her to come out, or that he had gone. This is utterly ridiculous, she told herself. Why am I so frightened? This is Simon for God's sake; he's just got it all wrong. Surely now he'll understand that he can't stay. He won't want to now he realises that I'm serious. Her thoughts were racing, scurrying round in her head as she tried to rationalise what had happened, and still she sat there feeling frozen, unable to move until there was a light tap on the door and Tessa's voice said hesitantly, 'Hester, are you there? Are you all right?' Hester gave a sob of relief and found her voice. 'Tess, come in please.'

Tessa opened the door and peeped in. What she saw brought her running across the room to drop down beside Hester, an arm round her shoulders.

'I knew there was something wrong. What on earth has happened?'

Hester stared down at her locked hands, the knuckles white with tension.

'I honestly don't know. I don't understand Simon anymore. He doesn't seem to have listened to anything I've said. He's just operating to his own agenda and deaf to anything he doesn't want to hear. It's weird.'

'It's weird all right. He was as white as a sheet when he passed me. He nearly knocked me over on the way out. I don't think he even saw me. That's why I came up to see if you were OK.'

Hester regarded her anxiously.

'Tess, what do you think is the matter with him? He's never behaved like this before. He's always seemed so gentle, sort of diffident. He's like someone possessed over this plan he's got.'

'I'm not a psychologist but obsessed may be nearer the mark. I think he's probably dreamed of this for years and now he thinks he can make it come true. Now he's got all this money he's free to do what he wants.'

Hester's mouth tightened. 'Well he can't do it. He's not taking over. Not me, not my home. I've got to make him see it's not on.'

They were silent for a moment and then Tessa said, 'Cup of tea, or something stronger?'

The prosaic question immediately brought normality and Hester chuckled. 'Oh yes, tea bless you. Just what I want. Oh Tess, I will miss you.'

'Well, I'm not gone yet. Not for another few weeks so lets hope this is all sorted before then.'

* * *

But as she went to put the kettle on her cheerful expression belied her private thoughts. How to tell Hester what she really thought was more than she knew how to cope with. She would just have to wait and watch. With a rush of warmth and relief she remembered that on Saturday Tim would be here. A sane and sensible presence among all these tangled emotions and she could talk to him and get his view of it all. Perhaps her fears were over dramatic and he would put it into perspective.

* * *

On leaving the house Simon stormed down the cliff path at a furious pace. Reaching the beach he turned up the estuary striding across the damp sand until he reached the wedge of water and could go no further. He sat down on a smooth rock, his head pounding and buzzing as if a swarm of bees were beating against his skull. He felt hot and sick, his whole body shaking. Why, why was she being like this? Why couldn't she see what he could see? Their perfect lives stretching in front of them, golden, carefree, no worry or pressure. Perpetual summer, everything he'd ever wanted. Just to be with her. They didn't need anyone else. Gradually the coolness, the stillness and soft lapping of the water calmed him, the buzzing in his head receded, his thoughts became less chaotic. A picture of her, as he had first seen her, came into his mind. The picture he'd treasured and brooded over for twenty-five years. A lonely, nervous eleven year old, he'd walked into the London sitting room, his father's voice behind him, hearty with false bonhomie.

'Here we are then, Simon. This is Hester.' And he had looked up into a serious, beautiful face framed in a cloud of red gold hair and fallen hopelessly and irrevocably in love. Not that he had been aware of it at the time. He just knew that with this person he felt completely happy and safe and properly understood for the first time in his life. He remembered how he wanted to be near her every minute of his visits. He would go wherever she was and just stand, silently, breathing in the smell of her, drinking in the look of her, fulfilled by her presence. She always treated him with affectionate interest and when they did things together she gave him her total attention. He had never had anyone's full attention in his life and he had found it unbelievably satisfying and exciting. His holidays were what he lived for, counting off the days like a long-term prisoner, and the day of his leaving her caused him physical distress. But he had never realised his true feelings until the day he went down to the cottage after Fliss's death. Until then she had been a dearly beloved mother figure, his haven and security. The moment he took her into his arms, her body shaking with intolerable grief, had been a revelation. He had been swept with a sexual desire so strong it had left him as breathless as a blow to the stomach. Shocked to his very soul by what he felt he had continued to behave as a devoted son, but gradually accepted his feelings and began to justify and then to plan. Nurtured in secret, unable to be spoken of, his desire expanded into unshakeable belief that they would and should be together, somehow, sometime. Now, the time had surely come. Anyone before had just been a game, a barrier to boredom and a brief sexual release. Even as those girls moaned and panted and strained against him it was her face and voice that filled his mind. It was her skin he stroked, her hair he ran through his fingers and at the shudder of their final orgasm it was her body that he entered and triumphantly possessed. With that thought he had a surge of cold anger. Jennifer. She must be dealt with and quickly. Sitting in the cool, salty dark he stared unseeingly ahead. The chaos in his head gradually subsided into a deadly determination.

* * *

Tim arrived on Saturday afternoon. A genial sunburned giant, towering over Tessa's five foot six, making her sturdy body look positively frail by comparison. Hester looked up into brilliantly blue twinkling eyes topped by a thatch of black curls and felt a flash of envy for Tessa. What an absolute darling, the lucky girl. Watching them from the kitchen window as they sat under the willow she could feel, even from a distance, the warmth and strong connection between them although their initial greeting had been completely prosaic.

He had breezed into the kitchen with a 'Hi there, I'm Tim' and her hand was engulfed in a vast fist. Tessa had turned from the sink to regard him.

'Well, Gog, you don't get any smaller.'

'Nor do you, Pud, nor do you.'

He had crossed the kitchen to stand beside her at the window one arm loosely draped across her shoulders.

'What a fabulous place. I can't think why you'd ever want to come home.'

'Might not bother,' she replied comfortably. 'Nothing to come back for is there?'

He'd grinned down at her. 'You've got a bit cheeky. I can see you're completely out of hand. I shall have to beat you into submission, that's all.'

She grinned back. 'Oh goody, when can we start?'

Hester interrupted them, laughing, 'Go on outside you two. Molly can finish that, Tessa. I'll bring some drinks out in a minute.'

Much later on Saturday night, Tessa, lying against Tim's massive chest in the drowsy aftermath of vigorous and entirely satisfying lovemaking, stirred and shifted away to lie against the pillows. Tim turned his head to look at her and laid a warm palm against her damp stomach.

'All right, sweetheart?'

She smiled lazily back at him. 'Very all right, my darling, just hot and pretty sticky. I think perhaps I'll have a shower.'

'How is the tide? High or low?'

'High. Why? Do you fancy a swim?'

'Yes, why not? You?'

'Excellent idea. Have you brought trunks?'

He grinned. 'Sweetheart, it's pitch dark and not a soul about. I hardly think we need to bother.'

An hour later, back in the caravan, cooled off, wide awake and companionably drinking cans of beer lying full length on the bed, Tessa said, 'So what do you make of it all?'

As always he didn't need to ask her what she meant, they had always been able to read each other easily.

'Lover boy and his step mum, you mean. Very Oedipus.'

She was silent for a minute then she sighed.

'I was really hoping you would tell me I'd been getting the wrong messages, but obviously not.'

'Fraid not. I can't get my head round the fact that she's so unaware.'

'Well, she's always regarded him totally in the light of a stepson. Until now she's never had any reason to see him any other way.'

Tim snorted. 'Bit odd, always coming for his holidays year in year out. Chaps his age would be going abroad, sun, sex and sangria and so on. He's behaved like a schoolboy coming home to mummy.'

'Yes, well I expect that's why she just accepted it. She's

so wrapped up in her restaurant and her own life she wouldn't think about it.'

'Very attractive woman but totally self-absorbed. I shouldn't think she ever considers anyone's feelings but her own.'

Tessa stared at him, surprised. 'It's not like you to make snap judgements. You really think that's what she's like? She's very good to work for, not temperamental and bitchy like so many chefs.'

He looked soberly back at her. 'You've been here nearly three months and she didn't even know you had a fiancé. What does that tell you?'

She said slowly, 'You're right. She's not really interested in anything that doesn't directly concern her.'

He downed the last of his beer and crunched the can in his fist. 'Well she's going to have to wake up and deal with this. I don't think it's going to go away just by being ignored. Time for kip, girl, you've got to be up in the morning. Come here.'

And that was the end of conversation for the night.

Chapter 6

Monday morning dawned, humid and overcast. Hester lay in bed feeling drained and exhausted, the oppressive atmosphere compounding her feeling of gloomy apprehension. Sunday had been distinctly uncomfortable.

Simon had not been seen all morning except as a distant figure when he came out of the gallery towards lunchtime and thundered away in the Porsche. He did not return until late evening and she was relaxing in her sitting room with a cold drink when he tapped on the door. She called to him to come in and he walked stiffly over to the opposite sofa and sat on the edge, not meeting her eyes, his face tense and set. After a few moments he said, 'I want to ask a favour.'

'Yes, what is it?'

'There's something not quite right with the car. I want to take it in tomorrow and get it sorted because I need to go up to Bath for a few days. Things to deal with over the house sale. Could you drive behind me to the garage first thing and then bring me back? Perhaps Tessa could if you can spare her.'

Hester was surprised into an everyday reaction.

'I didn't know you were going off but I'll take you in. Tessa will want to spend the morning with Tim. He's going home on Tuesday.'

'Right. Well, as early as you like in the morning. I need to get back to sort things out with Jennifer.'

He had sounded so calm and normal she felt briefly reassured. But today as she made her way to the shower, a little cold worm of unease settled in her stomach and she wished very much she did not have to spend any time in such close proximity with him. This is so stupid, she argued with herself, standing under the hot shower. It's only Simon, but somehow she did not feel comforted and the unease was not dissipated by his silence all the way back from the garage.

Within half an hour of their return the now familiar blue Fiesta turned into the drive and stopped in the car park. The girl got out, but before she could start toward the restaurant, Simon appeared from the gallery and strode over to her. There were a few minutes conversation and then he came back and into the kitchen.

'Hester, could I borrow the car for an hour or so? Jennifer is on her way home to London and we want to go somewhere quiet to talk. She feels uncomfortable here with everyone knowing what is going on. When we've finished she can carry on and I'll come back here.' His tone was quiet and reasonable and with relief, Hester told him to be as long as he liked. She would not need the car until the afternoon. With lightening spirits she watched the two cars disappear from the parking area. Simon seemed to be dealing with this in a much more rational and adult way than she had expected, perhaps he would try and let the poor girl down gently. She did not hear him come back but when she looked out at midday her car was sitting in its accustomed place and there was no sign of him.

When she went out in the middle of the afternoon he suddenly appeared beside the car.

'Could you drop me off at the garage on your way into town and I'll drive straight to Bath.'

He sounded perfectly calm and normal and she noticed he was carrying a large case.

'Yes, of course. Will you be gone for long?' Hester felt immediately uncomfortable, hearing the hopeful note in her own voice but he didn't appear to notice.

'Not sure, I'll let you know when I'm returning.'

He slammed the boot lid shut and took his place beside her turning his face to look out of the window, shutting her out. The journey was as silent as the previous one and he left the car with a brief 'Bye,' and disappeared into the garage. Hester drove away with such a huge feeling of relief and release that she began to appreciate just how oppressive his very presence had become.

That evening was the most relaxed and light-hearted she had had for weeks. Tim and Tessa arrived at the flat in the early evening windblown, sunburnt and happy having spent all day walking and swimming. Smiling down at her Tim said, 'Come on, get your posh togs on, we're taking you out to eat for a change.'

Laughing and protesting she allowed herself to be bossed and an hour later they arrived at an extremely famous and exclusive fish restaurant a few miles up the coast. Hester was entranced.

'How on earth did you get a booking here at such short notice?' she asked as they sat with the drinks overlooking the harbour.

Tessa grinned at her. 'We came and begged, told them who we were bringing and then there was no problem.'

At that moment the portly figure and gently swaying stomach of the owner appeared at her shoulder. 'Hester, my dear, an honour and a pleasure.'

She smiled up affectionately at the ruddy bearded face beaming down at her. 'It's quite time you came and visited me, Roddy. How long is it, must be all of a year.'

'I know, my darling, I know. Disgraceful but you know how it is. We celebrity chefs have such demanding publics.' The unctuous fruity tone was belied by the twinkle in his bright blue eyes. He patted her cheek gently. 'A bottle of your favourite in the ice bucket at your table, dear heart. Enjoy, I shall see you before you go.' And he rolled smoothly away disappearing through the door marked 'Staff Only'.

Tessa drew a deep breath. 'He's just like he seems on television only even bigger.'

'A right old poseur,' said Tim appreciatively.

'Oh yes,' Hester was laughing, 'but just wait until you taste his cooking, there's nothing posy about that.' By the end of the evening they both wholeheartedly agreed. They were served a delicate watercress soup followed by grilled lobster in an amazing buttery sauce, a melon sorbet to clean the palate and then a sumptuous cheese board. They sat long over coffee talking about anything and everything, except Simon and her looming problem, and finally drove home contentedly through the warm starlight.

Hester sat in the back listening with half an ear to the murmured conversation and soft laughter of the two in front and thought that she could not remember going out like this and enjoying someone's company in such an easy and uncomplicated way since the last time she had been with Peter. In a moment of clarity the narrowness of her chosen way of life showed bleak and cheerless and she realised it was quite time that she opened up a little and allowed other people in. These two young people had treated her as if she were already a close friend and she felt immeasurably warmed and comforted by their undemanding kindness. Impulsively she hugged them both as they parted on the steps. 'Thank you so much. It's really done me good. I didn't realise how much I needed a change and it's been a marvellous evening.'

They stood smiling at her. 'That was the object of the exercise,' said Tim. 'Sleep well, Hester, see you tomorrow.' And sleep well she did, deep dreamless sleep, waking feeling more truly rested than she had done for a very long time.

By lunchtime the next day Tim had gone and a rather subdued Tessa worked silently beside Hester preparing for the evening. However by the following day she was her usual calm and cheerful self and everything was running smoothly in the restaurant when Dougie the barman appeared in the kitchen doorway looking flustered.

'Hester, there are two policemen out here wanting to speak to you.'

Hester was exasperated. 'Dougie, for goodness sake.

We've got a full restaurant and I'm in the middle of getting the mains out. Tell them they'll have to wait or come back tomorrow. What do they want anyway?'

'I don't know. They wouldn't say. Just that they want to see you.'

'Well, if they must see me, get them out of the restaurant. They'll upset the customers. Put them upstairs in my sitting room and I'll come as soon as I can. Just explain how it is, they must see I can't simply down tools and leave all these people with nothing to eat.'

Dougie disappeared looking hunted and Hester turned back to the cooker trying to concentrate on the work in hand and not let her mind wander in speculation as to exactly what would bring two policemen to see her late in the evening.

After about three-quarters of an hour Tessa said, 'We can manage now if you want to go.'

So she did. Stripping off her stained apron she shrugged into the clean white jacket she always had ready in the lobby for appearing in the restaurant later on. The two men were waiting silently when she entered the room —one sitting on the edge of his seat, notebook on his knee, and the other standing gazing out of the window. There was something ominous in his silence and stillness and Hester decided quickly that placatory was the best approach.

'Gentlemen, I can only apologise for keeping you waiting but we are a small operation here and I could not leave the kitchen without the whole evening falling apart. What can I do for you?'

The man by the window turned to face her and she felt immediately uneasy. He was tall but quite slight with a thin dark face and watchful pale grey eyes. His voice when he spoke was a shock. Somehow she had expected the usual soft Devonian burr but it was a thin nasal accent, probably Home Counties and with a sharp insolent edge to it which was far from reassuring.

'Miss Hester Trent?' She nodded.

'I am Detective Inspector Gunnel. This is Sergeant Pederick. I wonder if you can tell me where I might be able to contact Mr Simon Brown?'

'Is there something wrong? Why do you want to get hold of him?' Alarm unfurled coldly.

'If you would just tell me where he is we will not need to bother you any further for the present.'

Hester was sharp. 'If you are expecting me to tell you where to find my stepson you might at least tell me why you want him.'

He regarded her with no change of his blank expression. 'I was under the impression that Mr Brown is not actually a relative of yours. I understand that you are not in fact married to his father nor have you been at any time.'

She was becoming angry. 'I have no idea where you have got your information from but although I may not have any formal relationship with Simon I have treated him as if he were my son for the past twenty odd years and I can assure you that's how he regards me. So I'm asking you again, what exactly is the problem here?'

For a few moments he didn't answer, his eyes steady on her face, then he said, 'We understand that Mr Brown has a relationship with a young woman by the name of Jennifer Thornton. Her car has been reported, apparently abandoned, on the cliffs above Mackerel Cove and she has not been seen by any of her friends of family or made any contact with them for three days. She told the friends she was staying with that she intended to meet Mr Brown and that is apparently the last anyone has seen of her.'

Hester drew a deep unsteady breath. 'I see. Well, I can tell you that she was here on Monday morning and they drove off in separate cars. I understood he was on his way home to Bath and she to London. As to where he is, I suppose he is still at his house in Bath.'

The inspector's gaze remained fixed on her face and she had begun to feel quite unnerved. He was managing to make her feel guilty simply by association with a situation about which she knew almost nothing. Then he asked, 'Was there any disagreement between them that you know of?'

Her thoughts were scurrying. Obviously the friends the girl had been with had told the police what they knew of recent events but it would probably have been a very biased account so there was no point in trying to conceal what she knew.

'I know that this girl had come down here especially to see Simon apparently to try and persuade him to continue a relationship that he had ended and he was not willing to do so. Other than that I know nothing about her.'

'I understood you to say you and he were very close but he did not confide in you at all about something so important?'

The veiled sarcasm was unpleasant but Hester could see he was trying to needle her into a reaction so she answered very levelly, 'I said I regarded myself in every way as a step parent. I have a very busy life as you have seen and he has his own life and friends hundreds of miles away. I probably speak to him briefly on the phone every two or three weeks and I see him three times a year during his college vacations. He is a grown man, Inspector, and no, he does not talk to me about his personal life except in general terms and I consider that to be perfectly normal. He would hardly come running home to Mummy at thirty-four years old when he fell out with a girlfriend.' She could hear her voice starting to rise and stopped abruptly.

There was silence for a few moments and then the Inspector said, 'If you will give me Mr Brown's Bath address and telephone number we will not need to bother you any further for the moment.'

Hester did as she was asked but when the busily writing Sergeant asked, 'And his mobile number?' she said she didn't think she'd got it and finally they went.

Hester watched them from the window to make sure they had left and then using her own mobile she dialled Simon's mobile number. It buzzed uselessly and eventually the tinny voice told her to leave a message. She thought for a few moments and then said, 'Simon, it's Hester. Phone me urgently.' She then left a text message to similar effect and slipped the phone into her pocket before going downstairs to check on the kitchen.

Studiously avoiding comment Tessa said, 'They're asking for you in the restaurant. We're OK in here if you want to go out.'

'Not really. They'll all want to know what the police were doing here but if I don't go it'll only cause more gossip so I better had.'

She stood still for a few moments deciding what to say and then, taking a deep breath, went to meet her public.

An hour later, her face aching from the effort of smiling and parrying the inevitable questions, she came back to the kitchen to find it quiet and tidy, Tessa busy sorting out the fridge and the rest of them waiting to go. Nobody said anything and gratefully she sent them off and locked the kitchen and passage doors behind them.

As Tessa shut the fridge door and stripped off her apron Hester said, 'If you're not too tired I'd be glad of your company for half an hour. I've had a bit of a shock.'

Tessa smiled the slow wide smile that Hester found somehow very reassuring. 'Of course, I'll make us some tea and bring it up.'

She found Hester on the big sofa, feet up, gazing out of the window frowning. Putting the tea down gently on the small table she sat down in one of the armchairs and waited.

Eventually Hester sighed and turned to look at her. 'I'm

sorry, I don't mean to be rude, but I'm feeling pretty worried.' She then went through exactly what had happened earlier and finished, 'So what do you think? I've left messages but he hasn't phoned back so far or left a message.'

Tessa sat silently drinking her tea. Then she asked, 'What are you most frightened of? I mean, what do you most fear may have happened?'

Hester gave her a small smile. 'That's one of the things I like most about you. You go straight to the point, no fluffing around the edges.' She paused and then said slowly, 'I'm afraid that she was so distraught when he made her understand that there was no hope that she... she's jumped off the cliff,' she finished in a rush.

Tessa nodded. 'Yes, that would seem the most likely scenario.'

Hester couldn't help laughing. 'Tess, you're amazing. Talk about saying it like it is!'

Tessa grinned back. 'Probably comes of being a farmer's daughter, no time for frills. Let's face it, we didn't know the girl, we can't pretend to be deeply upset. If she has done what we think she's done it's sad and shocking but we haven't done anything to contribute to it. It's Simon you have to worry about now. I mean until he phones, you don't really know anything.'

'I've left messages on the land line and his mobile. All I can do now is wait.'

But although they sat together for another half an hour until Tessa apologised that she couldn't keep her eyes open any longer and went off yawning to the caravan, there was no call. Hester lay in bed wakeful into the small hours, finally falling into uneasy sleep.

Chapter 7

Throughout the following day and evening there were no calls or messages. Another uneasy night followed and at eight o'clock the next morning Hester was awakened by a prolonged ringing of the doorbell. She went to the window to see who it was and was appalled to see half a dozen cars in the car park with two more just turning in. She had had sufficient experience with the press to realise that some story had broken that involved her because spilling from the cars were a number of hard-faced, black-leather-jacketed reporters of both sexes with the long-lensed cameras that only professionals carry.

The bell continued to ring unremittingly until she went to the box and switched it off and with shaking fingers dialled the local police station. They took ages to answer and standing well back from the window she watched the reporters milling around below disappearing from view obviously to peer in at downstairs windows and then moving back to look upwards at the flat.

With a jolt she thought of Tessa very much at the mercy of the rapacious lenses in the little caravan and was torn between phoning her mobile to warn her and continuing to phone the police. At that moment a tired voice answered and after briefly explaining who she was, and the situation, she said, 'I can only suppose that all this is to do with the young woman my stepson was involved with. Have there been any developments? I've heard nothing. If Inspector Gunnell's there I'd like to speak to him.'

The voice asked her to wait and there was a period of silence. Then a different voice said, 'Miss Trent, this is Sergeant Pederick. We will send someone out straight away. Don't answer the door until we come.' There was a hesitation and then the sergeant asked, 'Do you have any papers delivered?'

'Yes,' she answered. 'They are probably on the mat now. Why?'

'I think if you go and get them you will understand why the reporters are there.' His voice was sombre and Hester felt a surge of alarm.

'Please be as quick as you can. My assistant is sleeping in the caravan in the garden and I don't want her to have to face this on her own.'

'We'll be there shortly.' The phone clicked off.

Hester flew down the stairs and as she gathered up the papers her own face stared up at her. In the sitting room she spread them out on the floor. The flaring headlines said it all.

'Stepson of celebrity chef quizzed in suspected suicide' was the tabloids' version above her photograph, a very old one of Simon, and a publicity still of the restaurant.

The print blurred and wavered and her fingers were so stiff she could hardly turn the page to the inside story. After a few moments she thought of Tessa again and pulling herself together she started towards the phone when it began to ring. Tessa's voice said calmly, 'What the hell's going on Hester? Do you know your garden is full of reporters?'

'Tessa, don't try to leave the caravan. They'll mob you. The police are on their way. Have they found the caravan?'

'They have just. They are hammering on the door but they don't actually know there's anyone in here so I'll just lie low until the police come. The curtains are still drawn so if I keep quiet they will probably go back to the car park. Is this to do with that girl?'

'It's in all the papers, I haven't had time to read it yet.'

'Right. I imagine the restaurant phone is red hot; they'll be trying to get through. Good job you've got your private number as well.'

'They'll only get the answer phone downstairs.'

Just talking to Tessa was making Hester feel calmer. 'As

soon as the police arrive I'll get them to bring you over here and you'll just have to stay until the fuss dies down.'

'OK. See you in a bit.'

Hester turned back to the papers. The print had stopped dancing and she concentrated on reading first the tabloid reports and then the broadsheet. She had always taken two, partly because Peter's reports often appeared in the broadsheet and he had a regular slot called 'Frontline' which she read avidly. Shorn of padding and speculation the facts in the reportage were sparse. The police had made no comments except the usual 'Mr Brown is helping us with our enquiries' and apart from a carefully crafted interview with the friends who had accompanied Jennifer to the restaurant, pictures of her obviously distraught mother entering the police station and the cliff top where the car had been found, there was little else.

As she was finishing the second report she glanced up to see a police car entering the car park. After a few minutes her phone rang and when she picked it up a voice said, 'Miss Trent, could you please let us in. It's Sergeant Pederick.'

With relief she ran down the stairs oblivious to the fact that she was still in her pyjamas and opened the door gingerly, standing well back behind it. In a brief moment she saw a sea of faces and lenses behind the officers and heard the clamouring questions and then they were inside. She led the way up the stairs and turning to face them she saw the tall burly man in sergeant's uniform and an almost equally tall and solid police woman with smooth ebony skin and huge black eyes watching her with considerable sympathy.

In the soft burr of a native born Devonian she said, 'Miss Trent, you're as white as a sheet. Best you sit down before you fall down. Would you like me to make you a drink?'

Hester's knees gave way suddenly and she collapsed on

the sofa. 'Yes please, make some for all of us but first what about Tessa?'

'Would that be the person in the caravan?'

She nodded. The sergeant turned to the policewoman. 'Perhaps you'd better go with Jed and get her out. I didn't think there'd be quite so many of them.'

'Jed?' asked Hester.

'We've left someone downstairs to make sure they don't try and get in some other way,' he said dourly. 'If they can, they will.'

The policewoman disappeared and after a few minutes reappeared with Tessa, both looking dishevelled and Tessa's normal calm very much ruffled. She shook herself like an angry bird shaking down its feathers and said scathingly, 'I cannot believe those people. They're just a mob. Complete animals. It's disgusting you having to put up with this.'

'Price of celebrity,' the sergeant said testily. 'I think you'll have to give them something, it'll get rid of them a bit quicker.'

'Tea first,' the policewoman said turning towards the kitchen.

Tessa interrupted, 'I'll do that, you carry on with whatever you've come to do,' and disappeared abruptly.

Hester stood up. 'I'd like to get dressed if that's all right before we do anything else. I'll feel more able to cope with this with proper clothes on.'

'Of course, you go and do that and then we can explain what's happening.' The sergeant watched her go and glancing at his colleague, shook his head slightly and sat down to wait.

Flanked on either side by the police Hester gave a short interview of some three minutes. Answering the barrage of questions in a few brief sentences—yes, her stepson had been staying with her, no she did not know the girl in question, she knew nothing of what had happened until

69

now and she had no other comment to make.

Shutting the door on the clicking cameras and insistent questions she shuddered and the policewoman said, 'Well done, with a bit of luck they'll go, at least for the moment.'

Subsiding on the sofa and cradling the mug of hot tea with both hands Hester said miserably, 'I'll have to close the restaurant at least for today. They're bound to try and book in and probably attempt to interview customers. Can you please tell me what's been happening? I've heard nothing.'

The sergeant regarded her with a thoughtful expression. 'Mr Brown is being interviewed in Bath at the moment.'

'Helping you with your enquiries?'

'Exactly so. However he will be released this evening unless charges are brought.'

Hester stared at him. 'Charges? What charges?'

His gaze shifted. 'As to that I couldn't say. Perhaps you should contact his solicitor.'

'I haven't any idea who that is.' Hester was beginning to feel really panicky. 'How do I find out?'

'I'm sure if you ring the Bath Police they will be able to tell you. In any case, he might be released later on and he can tell you himself.'

Hester took a gulp of scalding tea and almost choked. 'I don't understand why he hasn't contacted me already.'

The sergeant was still studiously avoiding her gaze. 'He will have used his phone call to contact his solicitor. That is the usual procedure.'

Hester was silent and Tessa said calmly, 'Would you advise us not to go out today?'

'Most definitely, especially you, Miss. They would probably try to get your slant on what's been going on and just because they seem to have gone doesn't mean they have.'

Tessa looked at Hester. 'Would you like me to phone

70

everyone and tell them not to come in until further notice and cancel the bookings?'

Hester said distractedly, 'Please, would you? Tell all the staff they'll be paid as usual.'

The sergeant turned from the window. 'They're starting to go now but I'm afraid they'll be back. We'll wait until they've all gone and then you must phone the station if there are any further problems.'

An hour later the invasion was as if it had never been. Hester watched the police car turning out of the gate and turned to Tessa. 'I don't know what to do next. I feel absolutely pole-axed. What do you think?'

'Phone Bath police station, get the name of Simon's solicitor if you can and go from there.' She looked sympathetically at Hester's ashen face. 'Do you want me to do it?'

'Please. I feel really pathetic, I can't seem to get hold of myself.'

Calm and practical Tessa started to phone, first of all directory enquiries, then spending a long time being passed from one person to the next at the station, patiently explaining what she wanted and eventually passing the phone to Hester who had to reiterate who she was and so on and so on until at last they had the name they wanted. Eventually they reached the solicitor's secretary who informed them that he was with Simon but that she would pass on the message and ask him to call. Curt and guarded, her manner was far from reassuring and when Hester put the phone down she could feel her heart thudding and she felt sick.

'Tessa, why are they keeping him so long? What more can he tell them? If she'd jumped off in front of him, he'd have got hold of the police straight away.'

Tessa regarded her soberly. 'We don't know that she jumped off. We don't even know if they've found a body. As far as we know she's just disappeared so they're going to question him pretty closely. They're bound to.'

Hester got up suddenly and started pacing. 'I just hope that solicitor gets back to me soon. This is driving me mad.'

It was in fact only half an hour later when the phone rang. Hester snatched it up.

'Yes, hello?'

'Miss Trent?' A deep measured voice. 'This is John Hallwell, Simon Brown's solicitor.'

'I know who you are. What news? Is Simon still in custody?'

'Mr Brown has been released pending further enquiries.'

'Where is he? Is he all right?'

The measured tone did not alter and Hester wanted to scream.

'I have advised Mr Brown it would be unwise to return to your address or his Bath home, the reporters will certainly follow him to either. The police know where he is and I will inform him that you have rung me and are anxious for news.'

'Surely you can tell me something? The police here mentioned charges. What charges?'

The solicitor said smoothly, 'It will be best if you speak to Mr Brown. I'm sure he will phone you very soon. We just have to wait now while the police pursue their enquiries. No doubt we shall be speaking again. Good day to you, Miss Trent,' and the phone buzzed.

'Pompous prat.' Hester crashed the receiver down. 'Why, oh why doesn't Simon phone? Now I don't even know where he is.' Her voice cracked and she turned to stare unseeingly out of the window, her eyes full of tears of frustration.

Tessa was briskly practical. 'I'm going to cook something to eat. You've had nothing yet today and there's no point in starving yourself. You'll feel better with something inside you.'

Deaf to protests she came back some fifteen minutes later with a pile of fluffy scrambled egg and smoked salmon on thick granary toast and a pot of strong coffee. In spite of Hester feeling sure she wouldn't be able to manage more than a mouthful, in a very short space of time she was looking at her empty plate with a rueful smile.

'Tess, that was wonderful. You're absolutely right. I do feel better.'

'Good.' Tessa gathered up the plates. 'Drink your coffee and then why don't you go and have a long, hot soak. You can take the mobile with you.'

* * *

After she'd gone to the bathroom Tessa phoned Tim's number. His father answered and when he heard her voice he hurried into explanation.

'I've seen the papers, Tess, but Tim hasn't. He's been out all night on a difficult calving. As soon as he's back I'll tell him and get him to phone. Are you all right down there?'

'I'm fine, Pa. I just didn't want him to worry. It's all under control. I'll speak to him later. Tell him I'm perfectly all right. Oh and would you ask him to call in on my parents. They never check their answer phone more than every day or two and I can never get hold of them. Ask him to get them to ring me, would you, Pa? Bless you, speak to you soon.'

She put down the phone and sat very still. She was all right but she didn't feel everything was under control. Far from it.

Chapter 8

Hester was towelling herself dry when the mobile cheeped. Simon's voice sounded thin and indistinct.

'Hester? Hallwell told me you'd phoned. It's OK. They've let me go.'

Hester tried to sound matter of fact. 'Yes, I know, he told me. But he wouldn't tell me anything else and it's driving me mad because nobody will talk to me. What exactly is going on? Are you all right?'

He sounded deathly weary. 'Well, hardly, but at least I'm out. You've seen the papers?'

'We've had reporters here swarming all over the place asking questions but I couldn't tell them anything because I didn't know.'

'It appears they think Jennifer's either jumped off or was pushed.'

'Pushed?' Hester was appalled. 'You mean...?'

'That's right. They seem to think I might have done it.'

'That's ridiculous.' It was as if a cold hand was squeezing all the breath out of her body.

'Of course it is. In any case they have not found a body so it's pretty academic. She's a real drama queen. She's quite capable of going off and leaving the car just to cause this sort of fuss and get attention.' There was a pause and then he said, 'They want to know if I thought she might be pregnant.' There was a little silence.

Hester asked, 'And do you?'

He was emphatic. 'Absolutely not. No way. If she had been she'd have held it over me. I just have to hope she gets tired of hiding out and turns up and puts everyone out of their misery.'

Another pause and then Hester said, 'You really don't think she jumped then.'

He sounded scornful. 'No, not her. She'll turn up with some cock and bull story and then I will feel like pushing

74

her off a cliff.' He gave a little bark of laughter. 'Not that I'd better say that to the 'plod'. Anyway, I'm going to have something to eat and try to get some sleep. I'll phone you when there's any news.'

'Simon, don't ring off—where are you?'

'Best you don't know, then you can't be tripped up. I'll keep in touch. Bye!' And he was gone.

Hester sat on the edge of the bath staring at the phone. He sounded so sane, so ordinary she should feel reassured but somehow she didn't. Thinking over the conversation she realised it was his total lack of any concern that chilled her; as if this was not really anything to do with him just an annoying inconvenience that he resented being involved in. She got dressed and went downstairs to tell Tessa what had happened.

When she finished there was a short silence and then Tessa asked, 'What do you think?'

Slowly trying to sort her thoughts Hester answered, 'If all this had happened before Simon had come down this time, with his obsession about coming to live with me and take over my life, I wouldn't have even entertained the idea that he might have...' she hesitated, 'might have actually tried to hurt this girl but now, I'm not completely sure. He's not the person I thought I knew and he's behaving as if the whole thing is an irrelevant nuisance which I find, frankly, weird.'

Tessa said quietly, 'And how do you feel about him now?'

Hester turned away looking out of the window at the sullen sea. After a few moments she said, 'If I'm totally honest I wish he wouldn't come back. I'm not his real mother. If I were he wouldn't have behaved as he has and I would put him first, before everything else, as most mothers always do, but I can't feel like that. I'm selfish I know. I've arranged my life to suit me and I don't want it upset.' She turned to look at Tessa. 'Does that sound very dreadful?'

'No, not to me,' Tessa said prosaically. 'I've no children either yet so I totally understand what you're saying. In the last few weeks he's shown himself to be someone you don't really know at all. He makes you feel threatened and uncomfortable, almost frightened. I have to say I find his behaviour quite bizarre and I wish he would stay away too but I don't think he's going to, do you?'

Hester sighed. 'No, I don't, unless something did happen here he doesn't want to face. We'll just have to wait and see.'

The rest of the day dragged by. With no restaurant to prepare for Hester felt completely in limbo. She was suddenly aware what a set routine she had fashioned and how lost she felt without it. It wasn't until late afternoon that she realised that she had heard nothing from Frank for several days. Thinking about the flaring newspaper headlines she found this distinctly odd. He must have seen them and the whole village would be gossiping about her. Given their circumstances she could not phone him so would just have to wait until he made contact and, during the evening, he did. His voice was so quiet and exhausted she could hardly hear him as he told her that he had not left the hospital for two days except to go home to shower and get something to eat.

'She's got pneumonia now. They don't reckon she'll get through the night but they said that last night. Poor old love, you wouldn't think she had any fight left in her but she won't seem to give up.' He fell silent and Hester could find nothing to say except, 'I'm so, so sorry. This must be dreadful for you.'

'Worse for her, isn't it? Anyway, I'd best get back. I'll ring you when… when it's over. Bye.'

She put the phone down gently feeling the inadequacy of her response but not knowing what she should have said. How to comfort someone when they have accepted the inevitable? Bracing cheerfulness was out of the question and hushed sympathy seemed prematurely funereal and, in her case, hypocritical. She had never known or even spoken to Alice, she had been just a shadowy figure never brought to life in Frank's references to her. As she sat looking out over the darkening water she realised that here was another big change to contend with. Once Alice was gone Frank's life was going to be totally different. This was bound to affect their relationship and she could not be sure exactly how. What she did know with complete certainty was that she had no more to give to it than she ever had. It had always been part time and that is how she could manage it. With a feeling of vague uncomfortable chill she poured herself an unaccustomed brandy, sipping it slowly, feeling the comforting warmth spread through her body. Going eventually to bed she slept badly, tossing and wakeful from nagging, uneasy thoughts. She finally dropped off as dawn was filtering dimly in and woke to find the sun high and Tessa knocking on her door with tea.

'Sorry to disturb,' she said cheerfully, 'but it's gone nine thirty and you're usually up and about by now so I thought I'd better come and see. I'll go down to the restaurant. You come when you're ready.'

Drinking coffee together they looked through the papers Hester had ordered and saw that the coverage of Jennifer's disappearance had dwindled to a small paragraph on the inner pages.

'What do you think?' Hester asked. 'Should we open tonight or will the press come and harass customers to talk to them?'

Tessa sat quietly considering. 'I think we should open but you could do with someone on the door. What about your gardening chap, Tony isn't it? Would he come and do it for the evening do you think?'

'Brilliant. He'll be perfect, six foot two and built like the proverbial. He's always keen to earn a bit extra, I'll phone him now. I've got his mobile number.'

Having arranged this Hester was about to join Tessa in the kitchen when there was a tentative knock on the restaurant door. When she opened it she was surprised to see her visitor.

'David! This is nice. I can't think how long it is since I saw you. Come in, have some coffee.'

The thin stooping figure had to bend his head slightly to come in. Smiling down at her he said, 'I know, it's been a good while. Amy's not too well these days and we don't go out much. I'd love some coffee, there's something we need to discuss.'

She stared at him surprised but made no comment. Going to the kitchen door she asked Tessa for a fresh cafetiére and returned to the table smiling affectionately at the man opposite. David Taylor had been the architect who had drawn up the plans for the restaurant and been with her every step of the way as she fought to get it opened. He had since semi-retired and spent much of his time pandering to his petulant, semi-invalid wife. At first they had been regular customers but it became obvious that Amy resented their easy, comfortable relationship and had no intention of allowing it to continue, or become a friend of Hester's herself, and gradually the visits had ceased. Hester had been saddened at first but her life was too hectically busy to dwell on it and she hadn't given David a thought for many months. It was all the more surprising that he had turned up like this, unannounced, so she sat silently waiting.

'I don't know if you are aware that Simon has approached me to draw up plans for the conversion of the studio back to living quarters.' He stopped, watching her expression. 'No, I thought perhaps not.'

Hester could feel anger and apprehension in almost equal amounts rising up but she kept her voice calm.

'Simon is jumping the gun, I'm afraid. I have made it perfectly clear that I am not willing for him to take over the gallery but he seems to be completely ignoring everything I say and just pursuing his own agenda. It really is too bad. I do hope you haven't started to do any work on it?'

'No, I haven't. I have explained to him that permission for change of use will have to be applied for and that is down to you. Fliss had to do that before she changed it into a gallery and you would have to reapply to change it again. So he can't go ahead if you refuse to allow it.' He hesitated and then asked, 'Would it be such a bad thing, Hester? It would be a completely separate dwelling and it's a pity that it's left unused.'

At that moment Tessa came through with the coffee. Hester said, 'Tessa, meet David Taylor. He is the architect who designed my restaurant. Apparently Simon has approached him about converting the gallery and David wonders why I don't think this is a good idea. Will you sit down for a minute and perhaps you could help me explain.'

David looked politely puzzled as Tessa pulled out a chair and, sitting down, poured a cup of coffee and handed it to him. Regarding him soberly she said, 'I can see you think it odd of Hester to include me in this but Simon is basically indulging in emotional blackmail to get his own way and he's wearing her down. It's obvious from the way he's been behaving that he intends to try and control every aspect of her life and he cannot seem to grasp that she is absolutely not going to put up with this.'

David leant back sipping his coffee and listening with mounting astonishment. 'This doesn't sound like the Simon I know. He's always seemed such a gentle, diffident sort of chap. I can't imagine him trying to control anyone let alone Hester.'

Hester leant forward, tense with the need to explain

what was happening, to make him understand.

'David, he's very different now. Since he's come into all this money he doesn't need to work and he can entirely please himself where he lives. It's as if he's been waiting for this to happen and nothing is going to stop him doing what he wants. He plans to knock a door through from the gallery to my flat so that we can be 'really together' as he puts it and he talks about me not needing to run the restaurant any more but being dependent on him and we will go travelling together and not need anyone else...' She had gradually been talking faster and faster with her voice rising until Tessa covered her hand with her own and she stopped mid-sentence and sat back in her chair.

David, shocked into silence, sat staring at her until Tessa said vehemently, 'I assure you, she's not exaggerating, David. He seems intent on taking over and changing Hester's life whether she likes it or not. He seems to be completely obsessed about it and he's using clever tactics as far as other people are concerned. He makes it all sound so sensible and reasonable but this is Hester's home and the life she's built for herself, and there's absolutely no reason why she should give in to this if she doesn't want to. If Simon wants to live here in this part of Devon, there are plenty of properties for sale and as money's no object he can pick and choose.' She stopped abruptly, watching David's face which was registering complete amazement.

After a few moments he said slowly, 'This is quite extraordinary. I had no idea. Well, you don't need to worry. He can do nothing without your permission and if you don't apply for planning it's not going to happen.' He paused and in a completely neutral voice added, 'Of course, after this recent fuss and bother he may have changed his mind about staying down here anyway.'

Hester gave a short laugh. 'I shouldn't bank on it. He seems to be regarding what's happened as a trifling inconvenience and appears to be pretty convinced that this girl is just causing a drama to get attention and will turn up soon when the fuss dies down.'

David got to his feet. 'Well I hope he's right. It must have been pretty unpleasant for you. I'd better go. Amy starts to fret if I'm gone too long. Take care, my dear, and try not to worry. I'm sure it'll all come out in the wash.' With which comforting if meaningless phrase he ambled off smiling goodbye at Tessa as he went.

Watching him go through the door, Hester turned to Tessa. 'I'm just so glad you're here. If it weren't for you I'd think I was going off my rocker. I can tell even David who knows me really well thinks I'm overreacting. He can't actually believe what we've said.'

'Yes,' Tessa replied grimly, 'I can see that. Perhaps if this girl's body gets washed up somewhere they'll all change their tune.'

Hester looked horrified. 'You don't really think…' she tailed into silence.

'I don't know what I think except that anything is possible. I'd better get on or we won't be opening this evening.' Gathering up the coffee cups and cafetiére on a tray she went out to the kitchen.

In due course the evening went off without incident. The phone rang on and off all day and Tessa answered it, taking bookings and fending off the solicitous enquiries after Hester's health and well being which masked avid curiosity and giving short shrift to members of the press trying for interviews. The restaurant could have been fully booked four times over. By the time service was finished Hester was so nervous about going to meet her customers that she had decided against going into the bar but when she told Tessa she was going up to her flat the girl gave her a clear look and said firmly, 'I don't think that's a good idea. It makes you look ashamed or scared and you've no need to be either. If you hang on for a few minutes I'll tidy up and come out with you. If we're sitting together people won't feel so able to ask awkward questions.'

And she was quite right. Hester could not fail to be aware of the veiled, and in some cases malicious, curiosity but faced with Tessa's bland smile and watchful eyes no one said anything other than pleasant commonplaces. She closed the door on the last customer and said a fervent thank you to Tony who grinned at her and streaked off down the drive with a full-throated roar on his beloved Harley. Sighing with relief as she and Tessa turned off the lights and locked the door, she said thoughtfully, 'I cannot believe that I've only known you for four months. It feels like forever. Honestly, Tess, I cannot imagine how I'd be getting through all this without you.'

'Well, you don't have to,' Tessa replied comfortably, 'I'm not about to go anywhere just yet.'

The phone by Hester's bed rang at eight o'clock the following morning. Thick with sleep she answered and was jerked awake by Frank's voice.

'She's gone Hester. Four o'clock this morning. She just… stopped breathing. That was it.'

The deep voice was jagged with exhaustion and Hester tried to gather herself together to say something comforting and appropriate but could think of nothing except, 'I'm so sorry, so sorry.'

'It's for the best, we know that. She's had no proper life for years, none of us have. I can't be sorry it's finished. It's just…' A long pause and then, 'I'd like to come over later when I've sorted things here. They're moving her to the… to the undertakers. Her mother's already phoning the family. The house will be full of them and I don't think I can stand it so… is it all right if I come?'

His usual confidence was entirely missing and Hester hurried to answer in spite of pricking doubts.

'Of course you must come, if you think it's wise? I mean you don't want to cause any gossip at a time like this.'

There was a brief, tired chuckle. 'Oh Hester, do you really think it was all such a secret? Even her mother had a notion of what was going on. Anyway, I'll see you later.'

Hester carefully replaced the receiver, numb with shock. Had everybody they knew really known of their relationship? She felt as if in a classic nightmare, finding herself in an unknown place with no clothes on and avid eyes watching, running with heart thundering and terror in her throat until suddenly jerking awake in a familiar room, awash with relief that none of it was true. But coming on top of the newspaper invasion with the battering questions and clicking cameras she felt utterly exposed by Frank's calm assumption that they were public property. She had no guidelines as to how to deal with this totally unexpected situation. How naïve she had been.

* * *

Two hundred miles away a police detective inspector turned from staring out of his office window at the graceful buildings opposite misted by a curtain of drizzling rain. To his sergeant he said in a tone of extreme frustration, 'I'm bloody sure that bastard did it but if we don't find a body we're buggered. We'll just have to hope she drifts in further down the coast.'

His sergeant, large, fair and deceptively baby-faced looked at him curiously. 'Why are you so sure, Guv? She could just have jumped when he'd left, or perhaps, like he said, she's just trying to get attention.'

His superior snorted. 'He's just too smooth, too pat and too bloody unconcerned. Any normal bloke would be sweating cobs but not him. No, he's done something, I can't prove it yet but I bloody well will.'

Later that day the heavy swell of an incoming tide deposited the body of a girl onto the rocks of a small inlet

83

some miles down the coast from the cliff where the car had been found. It was not a pretty sight. The long immersion and the interest of various sea creatures meant identification would be a nauseating business but the long, curling red hair was unmistakable. In the afternoon a sea rescue helicopter spotted it and reported in.

Chapter 9

By the time the late evening news was being televised the discovery was being broadcast from every station but busy in the restaurant Hester was unaware. She had left the flat door open for Frank, hoping he would go straight up and not come into the restaurant. Deeply uncomfortable with the idea that people might be watching and gossiping, she did not want their first meeting after Alice's death to be public. Climbing wearily up the stairs she saw the sitting room light was on and he was there, so engrossed in the television he was unaware of her until she dropped onto the sofa beside him.

When he turned to look at her she was shocked. He had lost weight and his face was gaunt, eyes deep in their sockets and lines etched that had not been there before. For a moment she could see exactly what he would look like twenty years on and she was about to tell him again how sorry she was for what he was going through but he spoke first.

'Right mess young Simon's got himself into, seemingly,' and gestured to the television.

'What do you mean?' She turned to the screen and saw exactly what he meant. Numbly, she watched the pictures of the beach where the body had been found, police moving around in the cordoned off area and sightseers on the cliff top. There were patched-in shots of Jennifer's car on the cliff and the frontage of her own restaurant. Lastly, Simon being hustled from the police car into the Bath station with the announcer's voice rising and falling excitedly, 'celebrity chef's stepson Simon Brown—disappearance of the girlfriend—suspected suicide—body discovered—' on and on it went and suddenly she could stand it no longer and hit the remote control. The ensuing silence seemed more deafening than the previous noise.

Eventually Frank said, 'Looks bad, doesn't it? Bit rough

85

on you. Pity he couldn't have shoved her off a cliff in Skegness or somewhere. There probably wouldn't have been the same connection then.'

'You don't know he's shoved her off a cliff as you put it. No one's saying that,' Hester said vehemently.

'Implying it though. You haven't been listening to it for the last half an hour.'

'Frank don't, please don't.' She got up and walked to the window gazing out into the dark. The wind had got up and was soughing round the chimney and the scrubby bushes on the cliff edge were whipping inshore. Down below the phosphorescent wave tips gleamed and tumbled. The view looked bleak and forbidding and gave her none of its usual comfort. She turned back to look at Frank who was rubbing a tired hand across an unshaven face and felt immediate compunction. He had come to her for some peace and comfort and she was in no state to give it.

'Frank, I'm so sorry.' She crossed to the sofa and sat down beside him taking his hand in both of hers. 'What can I do? Would you like anything to eat?'

'No thanks,' he responded, 'I've helped myself to some brandy. I just want to be able to sleep. I haven't really, for the last four days. Hospital armchairs aren't the most comfortable.'

Hesitantly, knowing it was not at all what she wanted, Hester asked, 'Do you want to stay here?'

He turned and looked at her levelly. 'Not a good idea, the night after she's died. That would cause gossip. No, I'll go home. Rent-a-crowd should all be gone by now. The old lady may have gone back to her cottage, I hope she has.'

Hester was surprised. 'I thought you got on well with your mother-in-law.'

He gave a bark of laughter. 'Did you really? I think the only thing we had in common was Alice. Ma thought she

86

could have done better for herself than a local fisherman. She had big hopes for Alice and it's all come to nothing.' He looked sideways at her, a sliding almost malicious glance. 'Her suspicions of us didn't help. She's not going to be happy when we go public.' He heaved himself off the sofa and stood looking down at her for a moment. 'My life's been on hold for long enough. I did my best for Alice but I did my grieving a long time ago. Just get the funeral over and we can start living a proper life. Well, best be going.' And that was it. He went.

She had instinctively braced herself for some show of affection but it had not been required. Sitting holding her mug of now tepid tea it occurred to her that it never had been part of their pattern. Cheek kissing and handholding was not Frank's style. In bed he had proved an entirely satisfactory lover, if unadventurous, but the rest of their relationship came down to shared knowledge of mutual acquaintances, gossip about local life, discussing their different work and... nothing. She sat for a long time trying to order her thoughts. Firstly, Simon's arrest and all its implications and effects on her own life and, further down in her consciousness, the lurking discomfort of Frank's easy assumption of their 'living a proper life'. Together? She could not deal with that problem yet. Time to face it after the funeral, which seemed to be Frank's starting point. Two hours later she woke, stiff and chilled with the mug of cold tea upside down on the floor and the brown pool of split liquid well soaked into the carpet. Too weary to care she went to bed and slept again until the alarm went off the following morning.

Two days crawled by. Hester was as busy as ever but her mind kept sneaking back to her problems. Simon then Frank, backwards and forwards, unable to concentrate properly either on them or her cooking. She burnt sauce, overcooked vegetables and undercooked meat but no one said a word. She became totally frustrated and angry with herself but could resolve nothing, tense with waiting for the phone to ring.

Reporters had arrived the first morning and remembering the previous police advice she had allowed them into the restaurant and with Tessa standing grimly beside her had given a short statement. No, she had not spoken to Simon. No, she had not seen him. She knew nothing except what she had seen on the television. She had no idea what was happening or when he might be released or come back. To the more searching questions about his relationship with Jennifer she said she had never met her and she had no comment to make. Finally they put their notebooks disappointedly away and filed out. She felt sure that some of them booked into the restaurant but for the last two evenings she had not appeared in the bar and she heard nothing further.

Another two days passed with no word from Simon but on the second evening, as she was relaxing in the flat at the end of service, the phone rang.

'Hester?' His voice was thin and crackly with static.

'Where are you?'

'Still in Bath. Dreadful reception here. They let me go. Again. They haven't charged me with anything.'

'Thank God for that. Is that it?'

A weary sigh. 'Oh no. Further enquiries pending apparently. They've found nothing whatever to link me to Jennifer's death, although that bastard Inspector is certainly trying hard enough.'

'Well, they won't, will they? You weren't there when… well… when she jumped, or whatever.'

'Exactly. But her mother's kicking up a hell of a fuss, saying Jennifer was happy and well-balanced, and would never… etcetera, di da, di da.' In spite of the static crackle the contempt in his voice was clear. 'Well-balanced is not how I would put it. Neurotic little drama queen is more like it.'

Hester was silent, unable to think of any reply to this arrogant dismissal of a life in which he had been, however briefly, involved.

'You still there?'

'Yes, of course I am. Are you thinking of coming back yet?'

'Not at the moment, I'm keeping my head down, these reporters are an absolute bloody menace.'

'Are you at the house?'

'The house was sold last week. No, I'm going out of Bath. No point in telling you where, you can reach me on the mobile. I'll be back as soon as I can and when they'll leave us alone. Speak to you soon. Bye.' Click. Silence.

Relief washed over Hester. Thinking over the phone call she realised it was more at the idea of his continued absence than anything else. She slept better that night than she had for a long time but her peace was not to last much longer.

The phone by the bed rang early next morning. Frank said, 'Is it OK if I come over tomorrow evening? Funeral's three o'clock today. Best I don't come tonight, it wouldn't look too good. And Ma's organising a right "do" for afterwards, digging relatives out of the woodwork who haven't bothered with Alice for years. Makes me sick, they'll all be weeping and wailing and saying how sad it is and I'll bet they can't even remember what she looked like. Families!' His voice was sharp and bitter.

Hester said soothingly, 'It probably makes your mother-in-law feel better, like Alice's life was not a complete waste and that people will remember her.'

He sighed. 'I suppose so. Anyway, this is the last of it. I'm going to put the cottage on the market as soon as. Should get a good price, they're being snapped up by second-homers. And it'll all be profit, I've no mortgage.'

Hester felt a creeping chill. 'So where do you plan to live?' she said carefully. Silence stretched and her stomach dipped. 'Frank?'

His voice was cold and quiet. 'I thought that was pretty much settled. Unless, of course, if you think the flat is too small for two of us, we could use the money from the cottage to extend into the studio and that would put the stopper on Simon's little games. That is, if he's not doing a stretch for murder. What's happening by the way?'

Hester tried to rein in her galloping thoughts. 'They've let him go. No charge. He'll be back soon.'

'Just as well if we get everything sorted out as soon as possible so he can see that he's got to make other arrangements.'

A slow anger began to burn in Hester. How dare he assume he could take over her life, just as Simon was trying to, without any reference to what she might want? Before she could gather herself together to form a reply, Frank said, 'I'd better go, I'll see you tomorrow. Take care.' And he was gone.

Hester lay in bed for another half an hour, anger and panic knotting her muscles and making chaos of her attempts to see a clear route out of a position she seemed to have been forced into.

Where had all this come from? A month ago her life had been safe, calm and ordered, and now two people she had thought she knew and had believed knew her and appreciated how she had chosen to live her life were trampling all over it. It did not seem to have remotely occurred to either of them that they were not only moving the goal posts but making firewood of them. Each with their own completely separate but almost identical agendas and she backed against a wall fighting both of them. It was a nightmare. I've got to talk to Tess, she thought and threw back the duvet but as she went into the shower she realised that Tess knew nothing about her relationship with Frank and Hester felt very unsure how she would regard it. Standing in the shower, she began to consider just how it would appear and for the first time felt deeply uncomfortable. It had seemed such a simple and uncomplicated arrangement, harming no one, but was this true? Even if Alice had been unaware, Frank seemed to have read far more into it than she had any idea of and she was certainly going to hurt him when she explained that he had been building his castles on the sand. And that, she decided, as she dried herself, was going to have to be very soon. The last thing she wanted was to face him with it while he was still raw from Alice's death but he did not seem to want to waste any time before starting his new life so she would have to stop him. Swiftly climbing into jeans and tee shirt she went down to Tessa.

Pouring her second cup of coffee she said, 'That's the evening settled then. It looks busy. By the way, Simon has phoned. He's been released, no charges, but apparently the police aren't satisfied and they're still digging.'

'How did he seem?'

Hester stirred her coffee thoughtfully. 'Difficult to say. I couldn't hear him very well. He just doesn't seem to have any feelings about it at all except annoyance that the police suspect him at all.'

'I see.' Tessa's voice was neutral.

'What does that mean?' Hester said sharply.

Tessa smiled at her. 'Don't bite my head off. I suppose I mean that I'm not surprised at his attitude. People with a single-minded obsession like him can't really relate to anything that doesn't impinge on it. Jennifer's gone so that's an irritating nuisance out of the way. That's all.'

Hester stared at her. 'That's really shocking. I can't believe that an obsession with a place can make someone so indifferent to people.'

There was a long silence while they just looked at each other. Tessa spread her hands on the table studying her nails and finally, letting out her breath with a deep sigh she looked up at Hester.

'You cannot really be so unaware what's at the back of all this, Hester.'

'What do you mean? It's all about his obsession with this place and wanting to live here and, basically, recreate his childhood. Isn't it?'

'With one notable difference.'

'What difference?'

'He doesn't want a stepmother. He wants a lover.'

Shocked into immobility Hester sat motionless. Eventually Tessa said, 'I'm sorry but someone had to spell it out. I think your friend Frank has recognised what's going on.'

Hester said slowly, 'It's weird. It's as if I've been trying to put a jigsaw together but the pieces wouldn't fit and suddenly the picture is all complete and I can see it clearly.'

She was silent again for a little while and then she said softly, 'Poor Simon; what a mess. How could I have known what was in his mind all these years? He's always been a boy to me.' She looked at Tessa. 'What am I going to do? I haven't the faintest idea how to deal with it.'

'With great care,' Tessa said soberly. 'Simon is completely irrational where this is concerned and now he's got all this money he thinks he can buy what he wants and do as he likes. I think you'll just have to stick firmly to your guns, that you prefer to live alone and always have done and if he wants to live down here he must buy another property and he can still see you.'

Hester shivered. 'I'm not even comfortable with that now I've understood properly what he wants of me. Still, I can't stop him living down here, so I'll just have to manage as best I can.' She sat quietly for a few minutes and then looked almost beseechingly at Tessa. 'Are you really sure about this? He never actually said...' she faltered and stopped.

Tessa said gently, 'Think about the conversations you've had since he came down, especially that evening when you were so upset, there isn't any other construction to put on it, is there?'

'No, you're right. I've just buried my head in the sand. Well, we'd better get on or we won't be ready tonight.' And that was the end of discussion. But as she worked she thought of Tessa's comment about 'your friend Frank' and wondered if his awareness of Simon's intentions were at the back of his determination to stake his claim on her with such indecent haste.

Saturday passed all too quickly; the looming confrontation with Frank was like a threatening thundercloud at the back of her mind. By the time she was reluctantly climbing the stairs of the flat he had begun to assume the ludicrous proportions of a child's bogeyman and the sight of his familiar stocky body comfortably at ease on the sofa was almost a shock. He turned his head to smile at her and stretched a lazy hand to clasp hers and she felt the tension drain away and a sort of relaxed warmth spread through her. After all this was only Frank, not someone in the grip of a fanatical obsession. She could talk rationally to him and he would understand. They would carry on living separately and still be friends. She didn't want to lose him, particularly now, with the problem of Simon. All these thoughts chased through her head as she dropped down beside him and he put his arm comfortably around her.

'A little celebration,' he said indicating the two full wine glasses on the low table. 'I brought a good one, or so the man in the shop told me. It better be for what it cost! I know you're not keen on white so I hope you'll like this.' He picked up both glasses and handed her one. 'To us and the future.'

They clinked their glasses and Hester took a tentative sip. It was indeed a good wine and she felt the deep warmth spread slowly outwards from her breastbone to her stomach. I shall have to be careful, she thought, I drink so little I'll be legless on a couple of glasses of something as strong as this. But the long exhausting day was catching up with her. It was so comfortable sitting there, as so often they had done before, her feet up across Frank's knees, the window open to the warm dark and the soft brushing whisper of the sea below. The level in the wine bottle slowly lowered as they talked, easily, with equally easy silences. He told her about the funeral, making her laugh with his descriptions of some of the ancient relatives and their banal expressions of sympathy. The spiky bitterness of the previous day had dissipated and he seemed to have arrived at a resigned acceptance of everything that had happened.

Sleepy and lulled by the wine and Frank's soft Devonian voice, rising and falling, she didn't really pay attention to the content of what he was saying or the inferences to be drawn from his frequent references to the future. She was more than half asleep when he made his first tentative overture and it just seemed a natural progression of the whole relaxed evening. The sensation of his mouth moving softly over her face and neck and his big, roughened hands knowing from long association exactly how and where to touch to elicit responses were so familiar a feeling that she let herself drift, sinking into comfort and pleasure without thought. Eventually with murmurs and soft laughter they slid off the sofa onto the big white rug and he entered her. At first he was careful, moving to her rhythm, holding back for her pleasure, but when he felt her deep internal muscles contract and heard her gasp, all his pent-up need and frustration exploded in a rough, almost desperate coupling that left them both spent and exhausted. She was almost asleep when he murmured in her ear,

'I think we'd be better off in bed. This floor'll be a bit hard by the morning. Come on, my girl, up with you.' So to bed they went.

Chapter 10

Hester was asleep again immediately but sometime around dawn she woke suddenly, heart thumping, staring through the half dark at the bedroom door. She had the strongest feeling that it had just closed, she would have sworn she heard the click as it latched, but that was impossible, there was no one else in the house. She started to drift again but was jerked awake by the distant slam of a door and within moments the throb of a powerful engine, the rattle of gravel and the diminishing roar as a car drove away.

She sat bolt upright in bed. Oh my God, Simon. He must have been here; he must have looked in and seen us. How awful. How absolutely dreadful. Her thoughts were scurrying, her stomach knotting, she couldn't lie there any longer. She crept stealthily out of bed making sure she did not disturb Frank. She did not want to have to make any sort of conversation until she had thought this out.

Curled up on the sofa with a mug of tea she tried to calm down and order her thoughts.

'Get a grip,' she said to herself. 'There's nothing you can do about what's happened. If he's seen us he's seen us. Perhaps it's no bad thing, it might make him realise that he's been living in a dream and he's got no chance with me.' But somehow this did not comfort her. As so often lately she felt as if she were treading a very unsafe and dangerous path with no clear idea of where it was leading. And then there was Frank.

What was she going to do about that? Last night had been unbelievably stupid and selfish, she thought sadly. What on earth did she think she was doing? What had happened would only strengthen his belief that they had a future together and it would be harder than ever to convince him otherwise. If only he would be content to carry on as they were. She did not really want to lose him altogether but somehow she didn't think he was going to settle for that. So there would be more confrontation, more hurt, more anger. She sighed, drinking the last of the tea, and stretching her cramped muscles. She would just have to try to convince him that she did still care for him but she didn't want to live with him. Or anyone. What if it was Peter? said a little voice in the back of her mind but, sharply dismissing that rogue thought, she went to shower.

He came into the sitting room stretching and yawning, rubbing his hand over his unshaven chin. 'Any tea going, sweetheart? I've got a mouth like the bottom of a parrot's cage.'

'I'll make it,' she replied. 'Do you want breakfast?'

'No, just tea. I'll do something at the cottage later. I don't suppose you've got a razor of any sort?'

'Only the one I shave my legs with. You're welcome, but I don't think it'll do a very good job.'

'No, I'll leave it until I get home.' He followed her into the kitchen coming up behind her as she switched on the kettle, wrapping his arms around her waist, his chin against her hair. 'I'll bring my own kit over this evening and some clothes. Saves having to go to the cottage all the time.'

Hester's heart sank. She would have to spell it out here and now; he was leaving her no choice. She finished making the tea and they went back to the sitting room. She chose an uncomfortable upright chair to sit on at which Frank's eyebrows rose and he patted the sofa beside him.

She shook her head and took a deep breath.

'Frank. Have I ever said I wanted to live with you? Have we ever vaguely discussed it?'

He put his cup carefully on the table beside him and sat back watching her face, his own hardening.

'I don't like the sound of this. What are you trying to say?'

'No, you answer first. Have we?'

'Well, not in so many words, we couldn't under the circumstances. But it was always understood that one

96

day... well... when I was free that we would set up together.'

'I never understood that. Why would you suppose that there was any long term plan? Surely, if it was something we both wanted we would at least have mentioned it. If you want to be with someone even if it's impossible you would discuss it, dream about it, wouldn't you?'

He looked completely nonplussed for a few moments while he watched her. When he spoke again his voice was very cold.

'Even if your wife is dying you don't discuss what you'll do when she's gone. It's not... decent. It's like you were looking forward to it.' He paused, thinking. 'Are you telling me that you were perfectly happy with the way things were, that you've never wanted any more?'

She leant forward, eager to make him understand, to agree. 'Yes, that's exactly what I'm saying. It was perfect for both of us; we each had our separate lives but came together when we wanted to. I just don't want to change anything.' She was almost pleading with him. 'Obviously we can spend more time together now which will be lovely. You can stay over more often and we don't have to hide and creep about but...' She faltered and then braced herself. 'I don't want to live with anyone full-time, even you. I never have, I just can't face it.'

There was a terrible silence. Frank finally got up from the sofa and walked over to the window standing with his back to her for some time. She wanted desperately to break the silence but could think of nothing to say so she waited. Eventually he spoke, his voice very quiet and heavy. 'You say it was perfect. Well, perhaps it was for you. You obviously never thought about it from my point of view. Day in, day out, nights as well. Watching someone you've loved turn into little more than a vegetable. Not knowing how long it would go on...' His voice cracked and stopped. Hester waited, hardly breathing, and then he continued. 'I wished her dead so many times, for both of us. That'll be with me always, wishing her dead, my own wife.'

He turned suddenly, his face livid with anger. 'You know what kept me going? In those long nights listening to her struggling to breathe? You did. The thought of how it would be one day. Us, together.'

Stricken, she looked up at him. His face blurred and wavered through her sudden tears. Her throat was so thick she could hardly speak. 'I didn't know. How could I? I'm so, so sorry.'

'Sorry!' He was shouting now. 'Sorry! You're telling me that it was all a pipe dream, that we've got no future because you are too bloody selfish to share your life. You are a selfish bitch, Hester. Do you ever think of anyone but yourself?' He sat down suddenly on the sofa, his head in his hands.

Horrified at his anger she was unable to answer. She wanted desperately to say something to comfort him, to ease this dreadful disappointment but she could think of nothing. What he wanted she could not give. Perhaps she was just a selfish bitch but she could not pretend to a feeling she did not have.

Eventually he raised his head and looked at her. She was appalled to see tears on his face and unthinkingly she stretched out her hand to him. He did not move, just looked at her hand until she let it drop. Then he looked into her face, his own so haggard and desolate she felt her own tears spring again.

'So that's it, is it? This is the end.'

She lurched into speech. 'No, not the end. It doesn't have to be. We can still see each other, spend time together, just not,' she swallowed, 'not live together.'

He got up slowly still watching her. 'I don't think so. I want a proper life now, a woman to come home to, hot meals, a warm bed, some comfort and happiness. I've been a bloody fool thinking you would ever give me that.' He was jeering now, all his sick misery and anger concentrated on hurting her as she had hurt him. 'The high flying T.V. chef, aren't you? Not good enough to be seen with in public, am I? Just your bit of rough, eh? All right for a fuck but wouldn't do for a husband. Like I said, Hester, you're a selfish cow and I wouldn't stay now if you asked me.'

He came and stood over her and she shrank back, huddling against the chair. 'Oh, don't worry. I've never hit a woman in my life, and I'm not starting now. But someone should give you a good hiding, perhaps someone will. You won't get away with treating people like this all your life.' And then he was gone, striding out of the room, slamming the door behind him.

She stayed where she was, motionless, until she heard the pickup drive away. She felt paralysed, numb, the room still seemed to be vibrating with the furious misery of the man who had just left it. Gradually, like pins and needles in a cramped limb, feeling began to seep back but she couldn't think properly. What had she done? Lost a friend, a companion, a lover and revealed someone she hardly recognised, who in turn had turned a sharp light on to the person she believed herself to be. Shaken to the core his words churned around in her head. Was she so cold, selfish and insensitive? Did she really care more about appearance and reputation than loyalty and the feelings of others? Gradually her mind became calmer, less chaotic and she became coldly analytical.

Insensitive? Maybe. Perhaps she should have appreciated earlier how much Frank had believed in a future together, but there had never seemed any need to spell out her fear of permanent commitment because any decisions had always been rooted in a distant and uncertain future. Selfish? Yes, possibly, if selfish was managing her own life without reference to other people.

She had never deliberately hurt anyone but somehow she seemed to be managing it without intention. Care for her reputation? Yes, she cared deeply about that but she knew without doubt that had she truly loved Frank all such reservations would have gone by the board. But that was the crux of the whole thing. Affection, attraction, mutual need and pleasure in each other's company and a shared interest in their local lives and friends, those were the things that had bound them together, with the added spice of secrecy and enforced periods of separation. Through her feeling of loss and desolation came the undeniable certainty that this relationship would never have lasted so long without the necessity of concealment. The requirement to make a commitment would have surfaced years ago and it would have killed the relationship at that point. For a long time she had been able to have it both ways and now that was at an end. She was back to where she had always basically been, emotionally on her own.

A knock on the door roused her and Tessa's face appeared, not wearing its usual cheerful expression. Tersely she said, 'Hester, you'd better come down stairs, we've got a problem.'

When Hester reached the kitchen it wasn't necessary for anyone to explain to her what was wrong. Several cracks had appeared in the ceiling over the cooker and water was dripping through at an alarming rate. Most disturbing of all it was running down the strip light fitting immediately above it. For a moment Hester was paralysed. Then she snapped, 'Tessa, go and turn off the electricity. I'll ring the builder.'

Within a few minutes she was explaining to a rather sleepy man with his mouth full of toast that she needed him to come out immediately if not sooner, before the whole ceiling came down. Andy Harkness, the owner and managing director of the building firm she had used to convert the cottages into restaurant and living accommodation, was his usual easy-going, laid-back self. 'Don't worry, Hester, I'll send two of the boys out by mid-morning, we'll get it sorted.'

'Andy, I don't want two of the boys by mid-morning. I want you here by nine thirty. I've spent a great deal of money with you over the years and I expect some service. This is an emergency. I've got a restaurant to run and I daren't even turn on the electricity.'

At that moment there was a series of creaks like a tree falling and a large lump of plaster fell onto the cooker followed by a cascade of water. She held the receiver away from her. 'Can you hear that? The ceiling is coming down.'

A very different voice said, 'I'm on my way,' and the receiver crashed down.

Tessa said, 'Lucky I made some tea in the caravan before I came in. The kettle will still be warm. I'll bring some fresh tea over.'

Hester was still watching the water spread over the floor. As she stood there another lump of plaster came down and more water started flowing through.

'Perhaps we'd better turn the water off as well,' Tessa suggested and Hester just nodded. So aghast at what had happened on top of what she had just been through with Frank, she couldn't speak.

Within half an hour Andy was examining the damage and looking grim. This was more on his own account than Hester's as his was the responsibility for all the original work and all the maintenance around the place. He went upstairs to the flat and was gone for quite some time. Restless with worry Hester followed him up to find him on his knees in the en-suite shower. He got up heavily.

'Well?' she said sharply.

'I can see what's happened. The sealant has gradually come loose around the edge of the shower tray and the water has been seeping underneath and has built up. Because there's no way it can dry out, there's still water there.

We'll have to take an area of the kitchen ceiling out and the shower tray up then let it all dry out before we can repair it.'

'For God's sake!' Hester exploded. 'How long is that going to take?'

'Several days, I'm afraid. All the electrics will have to be checked for water, it's quite a job, but you don't have to worry. You'll get it off your insurance.' He sounded so calm and unconcerned that she wanted to hit him.

'Oh, and will the insurance company pay compensation for the loss of business?'

He looked uncomfortable. 'I don't know about that. You'll need the assessor to come down and look at the damage and then we'll get our estimate in sharpish. Best thing we can do is get the rest of the ceiling down under the shower and get rid of the water then there's no reason why you can't turn the water back on as long as you don't use the shower. But you couldn't anyway, because you'll have to leave the electricity off for now. I'll phone the boys to come over and start straight away.' He disappeared quickly downstairs, quite obviously eager to get away from his enraged client.

Hester sat down suddenly on the bed unable properly to comprehend the scale of the disaster. How long would all this take and what to do in the meantime? The restaurant would have to be closed for an indefinite period; she could hardly live in the flat without a bathroom and electricity. What an utterly appalling mess.

Tessa appeared in the doorway, looking at her distraught employer with sympathy.

'Come on over to the caravan. It's warm in there and I can make us a drink and some toast at least. Come on, Hester, there's no point sitting here. We can start making a list of everything you need to do.'

Unresisting, Hester followed her out and an hour later,

feeling marginally better for several cups of tea and slices of hot buttered toast, she sat back looking at the list in front of her.

'I can't think of anything else I need to get on to straight away, can you?' She passed the list to Tessa who read it through rapidly.

'No, that looks pretty comprehensive. It'll probably take you most of the morning getting in touch with everyone. What occurs to me is what are you going to do once you've got everything sorted? You can hardly sleep in your bedroom with a hole in the floor and you won't be able to cook anything without any electricity.' She looked questioningly at Hester who gazed blankly back at her.

'I've no idea. I haven't thought about it. I'd better get on with this first, then I'll see.'

By lunchtime the list was completed. The assessor would call the following morning, the butcher, greengrocer and other local suppliers had been informed, the staff had been told not to come in until further notice but assured they would be paid and all the bookings for the restaurant had been cancelled with assurances that they would be contacted as soon as the restaurant was up and running and each table would receive a free bottle of wine for good will.

Hester was leaning back in her chair feeling completely exhausted when Tessa appeared with a loaded tray.

'All cold, I'm afraid,' she said cheerfully. 'Cold beef, salad, French bread and a bottle of wine. I know you don't usually drink especially at lunchtime but this isn't usual.' She firmly put a wine glass in Hester's hand.

Hester smiled at her. 'You really are a life saver. Thank goodness you're here.' She took a deep swallow.

Two large glasses of excellent Chablis later and a good plate of rare beef and salad dispatched, Hester felt considerably more cheerful. Sitting back with the remains of her second glass she looked across at Tessa.

'I've been thinking. Why don't you go home for a few days? There's nothing to be done here so you might as well. I can phone you when the work is done and you've only got about a month left to work anyway.'

Tessa looked doubtful. 'Well, I could but what are you going to do?'

'If you go home, I could sleep in my spare room and use your caravan to sit in and heat up food and make tea and so on.'

'That sounds pretty bleak. Couldn't you go and stay somewhere more comfortable?'

'I could but it would be pretty expensive in a hotel, it's still tourist season and I feel I need to be on hand to keep an eye on what's happening.'

Tessa grinned. 'Keep whipping them on, you mean. Andy's not exactly Speedy Gonzales, is he?'

Hester laughed. 'Nobody is down here. It's part of the charm, except when you really need to get something done quickly. David was marvellous when we were doing the restaurant. He's worked with Andy on lots of projects and he just seems to have the knack of keeping him at it. He gets on well with all the men too.'

'I see.' Tessa looked thoughtful but said no more.

About an hour later she came and stood at Hester's shoulder in the kitchen. Hester had been watching as the builders carefully removed all the loose plaster. They had mopped up all of the water, moved the cooker out and brought in a trestle table on which they were placing a large industrial blow dryer pointing towards the hole.

'They won't be able to use that with the electricity turned off, will they?' asked Tessa.

Hester pointed to a long lead shaking out of the door. 'Generator in the van. It's plugged into that.'

'Oh, right.' Tessa hesitated. 'If you've got a minute I have a proposition to put to you.'

Hester looked surprised. 'What sort of a proposition?'

'Come up to the sitting room and I'll tell you.'

Upstairs Hester looked expectantly at her. 'Well, what is it?'

'I've phoned them at home and told them I'll be back tomorrow. Why don't you come with me?'

'What?' Hester was completely taken aback.

'Why not? You can't do anything here. You're going to be very uncomfortable. We've got tons of room at home. My parents won't take any notice of us; they're far too busy. It would do you good to get away from everything and no one will bother you up there. We're right out in the country and you needn't seen anyone if you don't want to. How about it?'

Tessa sounded so eager that Hester was uncertain how to answer.

'It's incredibly kind of you but I can't impose on your parents at a moment's notice and what about the rest of your family or are you an "only"?'

Once again she realised how little she knew of Tessa's life and how little she had bothered to find out.

Tessa chuckled. 'You don't know my parents. Father's up in London and all over the place. He's pretty tied up with the NFU. Meetings and such, and Mother, well she's a law unto herself. There's only one thing—' she hesitated '—are you very anti-hunting?'

'No. I don't have any firm feelings either way.'

Tessa looked relieved. 'That's all right then. It's Mother's raison d'etre. She's frightfully busy with the Countryside Alliance and she's always off to something. Both my brothers are older than me and both away so it'll really be just us. Oh, and Bunny of course.'

'Bunny?'

Tessa smiled. 'Mrs Rabbutt. The household revolves around Bunny. She's got to be seventy now but you'd never believe it. I suppose she's our housekeeper but she's much more than that. She's special.'

Suddenly Hester felt very tired. The prospect of leaving all the mess and problems behind seemed terribly tempting but how could she?

She said, 'Tessa, it's wonderful of you to ask me but I can't. I've got to look after things here, I can't just go and leave them to it.'

'What about David?' Tessa asked calmly.

'David?'

'You said he was in charge of it all before. Would he do it again?'

'I don't know,' Hester replied doubtfully. 'He might but of course he would charge for his time. I don't know if I could afford it. I suppose I might get that covered by the insurance.'

'Ask him. See what he says.'

That evening David came round at Hester's request. He examined the damaged ceiling and went upstairs looking thoughtful. After some time he came through to the sitting room and sat down, his expression carefully blank.

He coughed. 'This really should not have happened at all.' They both had the impression he was choosing his words. 'I would think Andy will be putting in as reasonable an estimate as possible. I wouldn't want to be quoted but I think the workmanship on that shower leaves something to be desired.' He paused. They waited.

'I'll be perfectly happy to oversee the work,' he resumed and unexpectedly gave a boyish grin. 'Actually, it'll do me good, give me something to do. Of course I'll charge but Andy won't argue that I shall be required on a professional basis.' He looked approvingly at Tessa. 'I think it's an excellent idea for you to get away for a few days. Things have been very difficult for you lately.' There was a small silence. Then he asked casually, 'Any news about anything?'

The softly closing bedroom door echoed in Hester's mind but she simply said, 'None so far. I believe Simon has been released but he's decided not to come back for a while.'

'Very wise,' David said smoothly. 'Well, I'll leave you to get some rest. I'll be down in the morning to meet the assessor and once we've sorted that out there's no reason why you can't go.'

Chapter 11

By lunchtime the following day they were on the road, driving their separate cars. After some discussion they had decided it made sense for both of them to have transport in case Hester needed to come back on her own. The assessor had seemed the most unlikely character for an insurance investigator. A jovial, paunchy man he had made no difficulty about agreeing that the damage would be dealt with under Hester's policy. He already knew David, which had helped considerably, and Hester was able to leave feeling reasonably certain that repairs would proceed straight away. With David there to crack the whip Andy's men would be kept at it with no chance to sneak off here and there to other jobs.

The traffic was heavy until Bristol but after that it thinned out and by the time they turned off onto the M50 they were making good time. Hester had managed to keep Tessa's little white Peugeot in sight all the way.

At the first junction Tessa turned off towards the Malverns and as they plunged deeper into the lush green lanes of Herefordshire, Hester began to feel a slackening of the tension gripping her. The countryside stretched away on either side, golden and peaceful in the afternoon sunshine, great old trees shading fat grazing cattle and cropping sheep. Nothing could be more beautiful and peaceful than the cliffs and coves of her own beloved Devon but this was subtly different. Wide and rolling pasture bordered by blue hills and chequered with farms and cottages, some half timbered and some in the distinctive local stone. It exuded a timeless serenity, a feeling that the restless world might be spinning past elsewhere but here the older values still held good. She noticed big hoardings every so often, with exhortation such as 'Beat the Ban. Keep hunting' or 'Support your local Countryside Alliance' and began to understand

108

Tessa's hesitancy over promoting her visit until she knew Hester's views. She was beginning to be curious about Tessa's home life but nothing had prepared her for what she found.

They had just driven out of yet another charmingly picturesque village when Tessa indicated left and they turned off through large stone pillars with a small lodge cottage at one side. About a quarter of a mile up a drive liberally scattered with potholes and lined by huge ancient trees they came out onto a gravel sweep in front of an extremely large three-storey house. Tessa continued around the right-hand side under an archway into a stable yard bordered on the three remaining sides by stables and outhouses which had all been converted into dwellings. There were several cars neatly parked in what were obviously their designated spaces but Tessa pulled up outside the back door of the big house and waved to Hester to pull in beside her. She got out and came over to open Hester's door.

'Here we are,' she said cheerfully, 'we'll go in the back way. I expect Bunny will be in the kitchen and we'll get some tea. Come on.'

Up a flagged passage, nearly tripping over quantities of Wellington boots and muddy shoes, Tessa opened a door into a room which looked to Hester the size of a small dance floor. An immensely tall thin old woman turned around from the cooker where she was vigorously stirring a large saucepan of something that smelt distinctly unpleasant. She regarded Tessa with no change of expression.

'You're here then. About time. I thought you'd got lost or had an accident or summat.'

Tessa crossed the floor and enveloped her in a rib-cracking hug to which she made no apparent response apart from waving her big wooden spoon and saying crossly, 'Mind what you're at. You'll have me pan over.'

'Don't be so grumpy, Bunny. I've brought a very special friend home with me.'

'Yes, so I heard. Hope she don't expect nothing fancy for her dinner. It'll just be the same like usual.'

Tessa stepped away to face Hester. 'Bunny, meet Hester. She's come for a bit of peace and quiet and decent home cooking. I'm telling you, she'll really appreciate your food far more than us greedy lot. I learnt more in this kitchen, Hester, than I did at college.'

Hester found herself being regarded expressionlessly from a pair of small black eyes heavily ringed with mascara in a deeply wrinkled face. Thick orange makeup, thin lips slashed with improbably scarlet lipstick and a fuzz of very black dyed curls arranged sparsely over a shiny pink scull completed an extraordinary picture. Her pin-thin body was encased in skin tight black jeans topped by an equally tight black T-shirt embroidered with sequins and rhinestones and the ensemble was completed by very large white trainers with flashing heel pieces. Hester could feel her jaw beginning to drop and tightening her muscles managed to smile instead.

'I'm really pleased to meet you, I've heard so much about you.'

The expressionless gaze shifted to Tessa. 'What you been saying then? Talking about me behind my back, have you?'

Tessa laughed at her. 'I just told her the truth, that you're the most important person in the house and without you everything falls to bits. You're the king pin, Bunny, and well you know it.'

'Hmm.' The old woman turned back to the cooker and moved the saucepan to the back switching off the ring. 'I suppose you want some tea then?'

'Of course we do. We didn't bother with lunch before we left and we're famished. Any cake in the tin?'

'You go and find your ma. She's around somewhere. I'll

110

bring tea up to the small sitting room.'

'No, don't bother. We'll have it in here at the table.'

'You will not.' The dispassionate stare came round to Hester again. 'I don't fancy being watched by no professional while I'm cooking. You go on. I'll have it ready in about fifteen minutes.'

They were dismissed. As they walked up the passage Hester said, 'Phew, she's frightening. I wonder how she behaves if she doesn't like you.'

Tessa chuckled. 'Don't you be taken in. All that is because she's recognised you and she's afraid she won't be up to scratch, which is rubbish because her food is fabulous.'

'What on earth was she cooking in that pan?' Hester asked with trepidation. 'It smelled very peculiar.'

Tessa pushed open the baize door her face brimming with amusement. 'Don't worry, that's not for us, that's Bessie's dinner.'

'Poor Bessie.'

As they came into the hall two liver and white Springer spaniels raised their heads from where they were lying and came bounding towards them with shrill barks of welcome. Behind them a rather overweight larger spaniel walked slowly but barking with equal enthusiasm. Tessa crouched down and they licked her face, bottoms wriggling and tails whirling like electric fans.

'Hester, meet Nip and Tuck and this old lady is Bessie.' She looked up at Hester her eyes twinkling. 'Poor old Bessie, her teeth won't cope with raw meat and biscuits now so Bunny cooks her up special meals. That's how soft she really is.'

Getting up she patted the dogs on their rumps. 'Go and lie down, lie down,' she commanded and they trotted back to the rug in front of the stone fireplace where a log fire hissed gently.

'I expect Ma's in the study. Let's go and see.'

They crossed the flagged hall scattered with faded rugs. Tessa opened a door on the far side into a small cluttered room mostly full of a vast desk with books and papers covering every square inch. An older, plumper version of Tessa was sitting by the telephone listening intently. As they entered she flapped a hand at them and after a few moments said crisply, 'Right. I'll sort that out and get back to you. Bye.'

Hester was aware of sharp dark eyes under a thatch of untidy grey curls regarding her with critical interest before shifting to Tessa and softening into obvious affection.

'Hello, my darling, lovely to see you. Good journey?'

She came round the desk to hug her daughter and hold out a hand to Hester.

'Delighted you could come. You must take us as you find us, I'm afraid. Always pretty chaotic here, but Bunny will sort you out.'

She turned back to Tessa. 'I'm out this evening, got a committee meeting and we're all going for a bite to eat at the pub later. Bunny will see to your supper. I'll catch up with you in the morning.'

'When's Dad back?'

'Tomorrow evening, sometime.' She turned to Hester. 'Er... do you ride?' she asked rather doubtfully.

Hester smiled. 'I used to, but not for the last ten years or so.'

'Well, you can get up on old Pandora if you fancy it. She's a real armchair ride. I expect Tess will be exercising Scimitar, won't you?' She looked at Tessa questioningly.

'Surely will.' She grinned at Hester. 'You don't have to, you know. You must do whatever you want.'

'I'll see, I might feel like it tomorrow.'

Bunny knocked on the open door. 'Tea, you lot, in the sitting room.' She walked ahead with a curious dipping gait carrying a very large tray precariously piled with china and food, depositing it heavily on to a low table in front of another fire smouldering in the grate. This room looked over the front of the house and the driveway they had come up earlier. The sun was low now, striking through the trees and gilding the leaves and gnarled old trunks. The view was pure Capability Brown and Hester went across to the long windows and stood silently looking out.

She did not realise how long she had been standing there letting the tranquillity wash over her until Tessa's amused voice at her shoulder said, 'Your tea will be cold. Come and sit down.'

She turned away with a sigh. 'I had no idea Herefordshire was so beautiful. I've never been before.'

'It's a wonderful county,' said an authoritative voice from the tea table above the rattling of the cups. 'Unfortunately it's being completely ruined by the government and their half-baked initiatives.' Tessa's mother handed her a cup, fixing her with a penetrating eye. 'Where do you stand on the hunting issue?' Before Hester could open her mouth Tessa interrupted.

'For goodness sake, Mother, don't bully her. She's only been here five minutes. I've already asked her that and she's entirely neutral.'

'Hmm.' Her mother folded her lips together and handed Hester a plate of warm, golden scones. After a few moments of obvious internal struggle, she said more pacifically, 'Perhaps we can change your mind while you're here.' No more was said on the subject. She and Tessa settled down to catching up on local news and exchanging gossip while Hester sat quietly eating the feather-light scones with thick yellow butter and homemade damson jam, followed by melting rich chocolate sponge cake. Bunny sat opposite on the very edge of her armchair sipping at her tea and listening, frequently darting inimical glances at Hester which made her feel vaguely uncomfortable. She was finding it distinctly odd to be sitting opposite this bizarre old woman in this typical country house sitting room: shabby chintz sofas, faded wallpaper hosting a mix of oils and water colours all dealing with either landscapes or horses, a profusion of rather dusty ornaments and some lovely old silver. Over it all was the faint bluish haze of the wood smoke from the fire and the creeping dusk as the sun slowly sank.

She wondered if it was the usual thing for the cook housekeeper to sit down to tea with the family, but the warmth, the gentle hum of the conversation and the delicious food were gradually loosening all the tight bands of anxiety and tension and she was startled when she heard Tessa's voice say, 'Wake up, sleepy head. Do you fancy a rest before dinner?' Embarrassed, she realised she had dozed off and started to apologise but her hostess interrupted her briskly.

'Nonsense, don't worry a bit. It's very complimentary when guests feel this comfortable. Off you go and lie down for an hour or two. Bunny, show Hester her room, would you?'

Silently the old woman limped ahead of Hester, up the shallow oak staircase and into another vast room. She switched on the bedside light and waved a dismissive hand.

'Bathroom through there, Jim's brought up your luggage, dinner's at eight, I expect Tessa will wake you,' and she was gone.

If Hester had been less tired the latent hostility would probably have bothered her more but kicking off her shoes she sank onto the queen-sized bed and enveloped in soft duck down was instantly asleep.

She woke gradually to see Tessa sitting on the end of the bed smiling at her.

'How are you feeling?'

Hester stretched luxuriously. Her limbs felt light and warm and her head clear and without the tight band that had been around it for the last several days.

'Absolutely great. What a fabulous bed.'

Tessa laughed. 'All the guests say that. It's one of the few things the parents will spend decent money on. Very important for people to be comfortable, in my father's view.'

'Only your father?' Hester enquired.

Tessa laughed again. 'Oh, Mother doesn't see the point of spending money on anything but horses. They, of course, must have the best of everything. Anyway, do you want a shower before dinner or are you okay?'

Hester glanced at her watch. 'Heavens, it's almost eight o'clock already. I'll just have a quick wash and come down. I suppose we don't dress for dinner in this mansion?'

'Don't be daft. Mother usually sits down in jods or gardening trousers. It's only you and me tonight in any case See you down there.'

Having disposed of one of the best steak and kidney pies Hester had ever tasted accompanied by four different types of vegetables perfectly cooked and followed by strawberry fool with homemade almond biscuits, they had moved to the sitting room with a tray of coffee brought in by Bunny. She thumped it down, brushing aside Hester's compliments on her cooking and left with a terse, 'I'm off now, see you in the morning.'

Hester waited while Tessa poured the coffee and then asked tentatively, 'Who exactly is Bunny and how does she come to be your housekeeper?'

Tessa handed her the cup with a mischievous look. 'I'm afraid you're seeing the worst of her at the moment. This family is very much her property and she's feeling threatened.'

Hester was amazed. 'By me? Why on earth..?'

Tessa settled back into her chair. 'She's an avid fan of your programmes. She watched them all and thoroughly approved of your traditional style of English cooking. As you see she's a marvellous cook in the old style herself, but

115

it's one thing to see you on the telly and quite another to cook for you. She's afraid we'll make comparisons and she's really on her mettle.'

'Oh dear,' Hester sighed. 'She is indeed a first rate cook and she's no need to fear me. I do hope she'll calm down, it's quite unsettling.' She paused then ventured, 'She's quite an unusual person, isn't she?'

Tessa giggled. 'You mean she looks positively weird. Yes, she does, but when I tell you her history you'll understand.'

'Go on then. I'm all agog.'

'Well,' Tessa curled her feet comfortably under her. 'Bunny was evacuated here during the war. She was billeted with our local farrier and his wife. They were a lovely couple, hearts as big as buckets. They had three sons and Mrs Rabbutt was really tickled to have a girl to live with them.'

'Rabbutt. Did they adopt her then?'

'No.' Tessa smiled. 'She married the eldest son. Her parents and grandparents were killed in the blitz and the Rabbutts wanted to keep her so she just stayed on. When she was twenty she married Martin Rabbutt but only after she'd been out with nearly all the other lads in the district.'

Hester was fascinated. 'It's hard to believe. I mean she's not exactly a beauty is she?'

'Oh you should have seen her then. Very attractive apparently in a thin, wild sort of way. She was a bit of a tomboy and spent all her time growing up with boys. I've seen photos, clouds of dark hair and legs up to her chin. She's always been different, made out she thought all Hereford people were clodhoppers, wore outrageous clothes and hung on to her Cockney accent, but it's all front. She adores living here and she's just as fierce about protecting our way of life as Mother is. She used to hunt but she suffers badly with arthritis now and so she just follows in her Mini. She's on the WI committee with

Mum, Countryside Alliance, you name it she's on it.'

'So how does she come to be your housekeeper?'

'Well, she and Martin never had any children and he died about twenty years ago very suddenly. She was devastated but they'd always lived with the old people and Mrs Rabbutt was dead so she carried on looking after the old man until he died a year or so later. Our dear old housekeeper had just retired and Bunny came up one day to see Mum and just sort of took over. Mum's hopeless with cooking and so on, no interest at all, so it suited everyone.'

'Does she live in?'

'Oh no, she goes back to the cottage at night. She used to stay over quite a bit when I was little, brought me up really.' Tessa smiled reminiscently. 'I spent my spare time hanging around the kitchen, it's what started me cooking.'

'She seems completely one of the family.'

'She's the mainstay. She keeps the daily women on the ball, the whole village is in awe of her, she's an institution.' She bent to take Hester's cup. 'More coffee?'

'Yes please.'

Handing her back the cup Tessa met her eyes.

'Don't let her bother you. Like I said, you make her nervous and that takes some doing I can tell you. Give it a day or two, she'll be fine.'

Changing the subject Hester said, 'Does Tim know you're back? You must want to see him.'

Tessa's face took on a particular expression that mention of Tim's name always produced. 'He's coming in later. He's on call tonight and he's had to go out but he'll stay the night.'

'Your parents don't mind?' Hester queried.

Tessa laughed. 'Good lord no. Tim's almost family anyway. Mother adores him and Dad think the sun shines out of him.'

Hester sighed. 'You're so lucky.'

117

'Tell me about it.'

Hester was intrigued but at that moment the door opened and Tim appeared, massive and beaming. After initial greetings Hester excused herself on the grounds of tiredness and went upstairs. The lamp was on, the curtains drawn and the bed turned down. The bedside table held an assortment of books and magazines and a tin of biscuits. Lifting the lid Hester saw that these were homemade like the ones at supper. Pulling out all the stops, she thought, Bunny certainly knows her stuff. She walked over to the window and pulling aside the curtain looked out on to the garden. Bright moonlight lit the parkland and as she stood there a large rabbit hopped out from the shadows and sat as still as a statue for a few moments before disappearing at speed up the drive. What a surprising day, she thought. I had no idea of Tessa's background but why would I? I never asked her anything. A vision of her mother rose in her mind and she smiled momentarily. Mother and Bunny, now that would be a confrontation. She imagined her mother's carefully plucked eyebrows rising and the immaculately painted mouth setting in rigid distaste. An expression that inspired so much dread in her as a child. Climbing into her delicious bed she leant back on the pillows allowing her thoughts to wander, remembering what it had been like to live under a constant cloud of her mother's mix of disapproval and disappointed expectations. A subtle form of bullying which had shadowed all her childhood and teenage years until that glorious moment of supreme rebellion when she had announced she was going to London to be with Duncan. How very different to the uncomplicated affection that seemed to exist between Tessa and her mother.

She wondered what Tessa's father was like and what was the dynamic between the three of them. Certainly unlikely to be anything like the uneasy atmosphere she had suffered. Her mother's overbearing social aspirations reaching into every corner of their home life and her father's silent, weary acceptance of them and retreat into the office and the garden. The only times she and he had been able to enjoy each other was in his garden shed seated on the two old car seats while they potted up his cuttings. Quiet, comfortable, murmured conversations inevitably brought to a close by some peremptory command from the French windows. 'Now, don't upset your mother,' was the dreary litany by which she had lived her young life. For self-protection she had expended a great deal of effort doing just that.

Lying now in this big, shadowed room with it's heavy, old-fashioned furniture, worn carpets and indefinable feeling of shabby comfort, it occurred to her for the first time that it was her own childish experiences that had made it so easy to empathise with Simon. She had never been as lonely as he. She had friends at school who had been allowed to the house if her mother found them 'suitable' but the emotional isolation had been very similar.

Chapter 12

That was the last conscious thought before she awoke to the rattle of cups as Tessa put a morning tea tray on her side table and sat down on the bed.

'Sleep well?'

'Like a log.'

Tessa poured the tea and handed her a cup. 'I'm taking Scimitar out in about an hour. Do you fancy coming out?'

Hester sipped her tea thoughtfully. 'I don't know. It's an awfully long time since I was up.'

'You must do what you want but it's a lovely morning and dear old Pandora won't give you any trouble.'

'All right. I'll have a go but woe betide you if she's not as docile as you say she is.'

Tessa laughed and swung her legs off the bed. 'I'll go and get them both tacked up and find you some boots and a hat. What are you, size seven shoe? There's everything in the tack room, bound to be something that's a reasonable fit.'

Hester finished her tea and somewhat reluctantly went to shower, wondering if she was completely mad to attempt riding after such a gap.

Later, seated comfortably on the back of an elderly and rather overweight mare plodding placidly in the wake of the skittish, sixteen-hand black gelding that Tessa was controlling with no trouble at all, she was thoroughly enjoying herself. It was a perfect September morning, hazy with slight ground mist, cobwebs glistening on hedges bright with hips, trees just beginning to bronze and a hint of chill beneath the warmth. She breathed deeply of the clear crisp air and felt more alive and optimistic than she had felt for weeks. The dark shadow of Simon's obsession she had banished to the very back of her mind. With the physical distance between them and in the golden peace of this autumn countryside it seemed unreal and almost ludicrous. Frank's defection was in the nature of a faintly aching tooth, a background discomfort rather than a present pain.

* * *

In Devon, David was facing a Simon he had never met before. Blue eyes glittering and face taut with anger he had stormed into the kitchen interrupting without ceremony the conversation David was having with Andy.

'What the hell's going on here?'

Both the other men were so startled that for a moment there was total silence. 'Well, what's happened to Hester?'

David found his voice. 'There's no need to shout,' he said coldly. 'As you can see there's been something of a disaster which we are endeavouring to put right.'

'Oh don't be so bloody pompous, David,' Simon snapped moving a step nearer. 'Where is Hester? I've been up to the flat and there's no sign of her.'

Involuntarily David had taken a step back. Simon's concentrated fury was positively menacing and he did not know how to respond.

Andy's lazy Devonian voice filled the gap. 'She's gone away for a few days, lad. No point in her stopping here, she can't even use the bathroom and the kitchen'll take another couple of days at least to be operational.'

Simon regarded him contemptuously. 'I wasn't talking to you and what Hester does is none of your business. David, where is she?'

'She's gone to stay with Tessa and what she decides to do is really none of your business either.' David's voice was icy. 'If she wanted you to know where she was going no doubt she would have informed you. Now Andy and I have work to do and I do not appreciate your attitude so perhaps you'd go.'

He turned away speaking over his shoulder, 'I imagine

you have her mobile number so I suggest you get in touch with her yourself.'

Between his teeth Simon said, 'Where... Has... She... Gone?'

'Somewhere in Herefordshire, that's all I know,' David said tersely. 'Now, please let us get on with the job.' He turned his back on Simon and continued his interrupted conversation. For a few moments Simon stood watching them then turned on his heel and left. After a minute they heard the roar of a powerful engine which gradually faded and insensibly they both relaxed.

'What the hell's the matter with him?' Andy asked, sounding quite bewildered. 'He always seemed such a quiet, easy-going sort of bloke. I can't credit him carrying on like that.'

'I don't exactly know,' David responded grimly. 'I do know he's been upsetting Hester with some truly half-baked notions and she can't seem to make him see sense. Coming into all his grandfather's money seems to have gone to his head and he's been behaving in a very peculiar manner. I didn't really take Hester seriously when she told me but I can see now why she's so worried.'

'Well, best she stay away for a bit and keep out of it and let's hope he calms down. All this fuss over that girl jumping off the cliff's bound to make him pretty edgy. I daresay it'll all come out sometime.' With which unlikely pronouncement Andy ambled off to instruct his men to 'get off their lazy bloody arses and get some work done.'

* * *

Riding companionably through woodland already carpeted with the first falling leaves Tessa said idly, 'Does anyone know where you are exactly?'

'No, and that was a conscious decision. David knows I'm in Herefordshire and that's all. Thank God for mobile phones. I'm phoning him every day to find out what progress they're making but that's all the contact I want.'

'So Simon won't know.'

'Absolutely not. In some ways this ceiling business is heaven sent. I would never have gone away if I hadn't been forced into it.' She turned in the saddle to look at Tess. 'I can't tell you how grateful I am. I didn't realise how much I needed a break from it all but now I'm here...' She gestured to the spectacular view as they emerged from the trees. 'This is so perfect.'

Tessa smiled back at her. 'Your Devon is perfect too but this is my favourite county. In fact, my favourite place in the world. I wouldn't want to live anywhere else in the long term.'

Hester said thoughtfully, 'I remember from your CV that you've travelled a bit. Remind me where exactly.'

'Well, I never did the backpacking bit that most of my friends did, you know, Thailand, Australia, whatever. I was always one-track minded.'

Hester glanced at the sturdy figure riding beside her, upright and easy in the saddle, capable brown hands firmly controlling the still-testy gelding and smooth olive-skinned face faintly smiling back at her. She thought suddenly, Tessa doesn't actually look English, more Spanish or Italian and the spontaneous friendly personality is more Mediterranean than Middle England, but she simply said, 'Go on.'

'All I ever wanted to do was cook, I spent so much time in the kitchen with Bunny in the holidays. Boarding school made me appreciate what a fabulous cook she is, the food there was so ghastly.'

'How does she come to be so good?' Hester asked curiously. 'She seems the most unlikely person to be interested in food. She doesn't look as if she ever eats anything for a start.'

Tessa laughed. 'She doesn't much. Her mother-in-law

was a great provider in the true W.I. tradition. You know, feather-light sponges, melting pastry and so on. Won prizes at all the local shows. "Her Martin" wasn't going to marry a girl who couldn't cook and Bunny adored Mrs Rabbutt. I think she was a far better mother than her own had been and she wanted to please her and then she found she had a talent for it.'

'Lucky you, to have her.'

'Indeed, we all know just how lucky. Ma is hopeless, always has been and Bunny dotes on my dad so we all benefit. Anyway, I finished catering college where I didn't really learn anything practical I didn't already know and did a year at a private Cordon Bleu in London, then worked in France for a year and finally Switzerland to really learn patisserie.'

'Why did you come to me? I thought you just fancied a summer by the sea.'

Tessa glanced sideways. 'Not exactly. I'd seen your programmes and I liked what you were doing. It is very much what I want to do myself. Small restaurant, traditional English food, I'd only worked in big restaurants with very large kitchens, up to ten chefs and so on. Your operation was small and perfect and I wanted to find out how it worked from the bottom up.'

Hester said slowly, 'So you want to open your own place?'

'That's the general idea.'

They were turning into a large field just below the back of the house where a row of purpose-built modern brick stables had been built with a railed concreted area in front. 'There something I want to show you later. I thought we'd go into town, when we've seen to the horses, and have a bit of lunch.'

Hester hesitated. 'I don't know, Tess, with all the publicity in the papers I don't think I want to be recognised.'

Swinging herself from the saddle Tessa looked up at her and grinned. 'I really wouldn't worry about it. Put your hair up and wear your sunglasses and nobody will notice you. It's a good few months since your programme was on and the newspaper pictures were pretty crappy.'

Hester sighed. 'I'm sure you're right. I'm just being paranoid.'

Tessa was absolutely right. Hester had taken her advice, screwed her abundant mane into a ponytail and was wearing nondescript jeans and tee shirt with large glasses hiding most of her face. They had lunch in the famous coaching inn in the centre of the busy market town, crowded with local businessmen, farmers, girls from the surrounding shops and offices and a fair sprinkling of tourists. Nobody paid the slightest attention to her and although Tessa recognised one or two of the people as she ordered drinks and lunch no one even glanced in Hester's direction. The only person who evinced the slightest interest was a very tall, rangy young man who looked vaguely familiar, coming into the bar as they were leaving.

'Hi, Tess, what are you doing back already? Tim didn't tell me.'

'No, Adrian, I don't suppose he did. It's only a flying visit.' Tessa sounded brisk and dismissive and Hester received the distinct impression that this was not an entirely welcome encounter. Tessa patted his arm as she manoeuvred past him in the crowded passage. 'Probably see you around before I go back.'

He caught her by the shoulder. 'Yes, but why are you back? I thought you weren't due home until October.'

'A few problems with my restaurant. Easier to come back to get them sorted than try to do it long-distance. Anyway, must rush, got an appointment in a few minutes.'

His gaze travelled indifferently across Hester's face and then sharpened. 'Hang on, aren't you...?'

'Excuse me,' said an irritated voice. 'Can you shift,

125

you're blocking the gangway.' A large, ruddy-faced man in cords and checked shirt started to edge between them.

'Bye, Adrian, see you.' Grabbing Hester's hand Tessa pushed through into the street. As they walked away she muttered crossly, 'Of all the people to bump into it would have to be him.'

'Who is he?' Hester queried. 'He looked sort of familiar.'

'He's Tim's brother and the last person you would want to talk to. He's a journalist on the local paper. Sharp as a whip and nosey as hell.'

'He recognised me didn't he?' Hester said anxiously.

'Probably.' Tessa was untroubled. 'Don't worry about it. You don't have to see him again.'

'But surely, if he's Tim's brother, you can't exactly avoid him. Won't he turn up at the house?'

'Not very likely,' Tessa responded briskly, 'Mother and he had a big falling out over an article he wrote about the Countryside Alliance. He's not exactly persona grata with her and he certainly won't come uninvited.'

'Isn't that a bit difficult, as he's Tim's brother?'

'Lord no, they don't see a great deal of each other. They've got a completely different set of friends. Adrian's always been a bit of a loner, the odd man out. He was a spiteful little toad as a child, always telling tales and trying to cause trouble. Tim's elder brother is a sweetie, just like Tim.'

'Does he still live around here?'

'No, he's a doctor. Married, two kids, lives near Derby. Tim's the youngest and the apple of his father's eye, bless him.'

'So Adrian's the middle one?'

Tessa nodded. 'Yes and that's probably why he's difficult. They say middle children often feel left out, I don't know why.'

As she spoke she stopped outside a bow-fronted

window full of coloured photographs. Hester glanced at the sign above.

'Humbert and Preece Estate Agents. Are we going in here?'

Tessa's eyes gleamed at her. 'Certainly are. I'm collecting some keys.'

'Oh. To what?'

'You'll see.' The suppressed excitement in Tessa's voice sharpened Hester's interest.

She waited outside, looking at the properties advertised and mentally comparing prices with those at home and realising that Devon was no longer that far ahead of the Midlands. When Tessa came out with a ring of keys they walked on up the street for a little way and stopped again outside another bow-windowed building but double-fronted and clearly empty. The sign over the door said 'Toreador' and from the faded menu card in a glass wall by the door it had obviously been a restaurant.

Hester looked at Tessa. 'Is this it? Your restaurant?'

Tessa fitted the key into the lock turning a glowing face to Hester.

'It will be. Come and see.'

Inside it was warm and airless, smelling of dust and disuse and still, very faintly, the scent of stale cooking. It was empty of furniture but there were old posters on the walls, generally Spanish and Italian travel type pictures and some very badly executed murals of olive groves and orange trees, a Mediterranean mish-mash.

Tessa stood in the middle with her arms spread and her smile nearly as wide as her face. 'This is it, Hester. By the end of the month it will be properly mine. I can't WAIT!' She twirled round several times like a small child, her excitement so infectious that Hester found herself laughing. In a burst of spontaneous affection she reached out and hugged Tessa.

'I know how you feel, I can remember just how it was

127

for me.'

Tessa beamed. 'I knew you'd understand, better than anyone. Come on, I want to show you all of it.'

The rest of the afternoon passed so quickly that when Tessa glanced at her watch she squeaked in surprise. 'It's five o'clock! I've got to get these keys back, the agents close at five.'

Driving home they continued their discussion. Tessa had explained that the restaurant had been owned by a gay couple, both British but who had been living abroad and decided to bring a more exotic culture to this very English country town. Apart from the fact that they quarrelled incessantly, although the food could be excellent on occasion, it was inconsistent to say the least. Also they had introduced some completely authentic Spanish and Italian peasant dishes which had not appealed at all to local palates, reared on the pub restaurant versions of tapas, lasagne, Bolognese et al. The inevitable had happened and the business had failed. The lease on the building would expire in three weeks time and Tessa could then take possession. The afternoon had been spent in going over the whole building while she explained in graphic detail exactly what she intended to do. The walls and ceiling were to be stripped back to show the beams, the plaster painted a rich terracotta. In contrast to the present stained wooden boards there would be olive green carpet and the small bar area in front would have deep soft leather sofas and low tables, old-fashioned oil paintings of horses and landscapes, bowls of fresh flowers—'None of your dried-by-the-yard arrangements,' Tessa said scornfully—and most important of all, the traditional menu.

'Nothing but the best English cooking. We've got fabulous local butchers and local veg shops and I'm going to have a good selection of local wines as well as French and New World. There are several vineyards in this area that have won awards and I want to encourage people to drink from them.'

Hester listened to her voice rising and falling, her enthusiasm and her vision so intense that one almost felt that she was putting out an electric charge and sparks would start flying out of her. The calm rather prosaic girl that Hester had come to know was completely eclipsed and she seemed almost like someone else.

They had finished their tour at the top of the building which comprised a comfortable flat: two bedrooms, sitting/dining room, small kitchenette and extremely exotic black and silver bathroom, legacy of the previous owners. Perched on the broad windowsill Hester enquired, 'Are you going to live here?'

'Yes, until Tim and I are married, then I might let it. It has a separate entrance at the back. I know Adrian has rather got his eye on it but I really don't want him living here. He's too nosy.'

'Where will you live when you're married? Has Tim got a house?'

'No, he lives with his father. It's a big house and the idea is that eventually his dad will have a separate flat in it and we'll live in the main house.'

'Plenty of room for kids then,' Hester said with a twinkle.

'Oh yes,' Tessa answered composedly. 'Not yet awhile but we both want a family.'

Hester felt rather a momentary stab of pure envy. Tessa's picture looked so sunny and settled, absolutely idyllic. She said abruptly, 'You don't mind sharing with the old people then?'

Even to herself her voice sounded harsh and Tessa's surprise was obvious. After a pause she said quietly, 'It's only Tim's dad, his mother died five years ago. In fact he's recently been diagnosed with Parkinson's so he'll need us there to look after him eventually.'

A small jealous impulse impelled Hester to ask, 'So

how's this all to be financed? Starting a restaurant is a very risky, expensive business and if you have to take out a big loan it can be a killer, but perhaps I shouldn't ask.'

Tessa glanced at her face warily but she answered readily enough. 'I'm very lucky, my grandmother died last year and left me quite a bit. Certainly enough to get this off the ground and help me through the initial stages. How about you? How did you manage?'

Remembering Fliss and the overwhelming relief she had felt when she realised that she could totally change her life Hester was suddenly ashamed of herself.

'I was lucky like you, my aunt left me everything and that's why I could start. I'm sorry, Tessa, I didn't mean to sound so bitchy. It was just...' She stopped trying to find the right words. 'You seem to have it all. It's not that I grudge you that, if anybody should it's you. I just—' She stopped again, unable to explain exactly how she felt.

Tessa reached over and touched her knee. 'If I should ever be half as successful as you I'll consider myself bloody lucky. Anyway what would you want with a husband, an ailing father-in-law and a possible brood of kids? You'd hate it!'

Hester smiled back, the brief unease between them dispelled. 'You're absolutely right. Domesticity is not for me. I found that out a long time ago.'

Now they were driving back through the early evening light, sunshine striking low through the trees, still desultorily discussing the restaurant plans, when Tessa frowned and changed down, indicating left and watching her rear-view mirror. They drove ever more slowly until Hester asked, 'What's the matter? Why are you indicating left when there's no turning?'

'There's a motorbike behind. He must want to pass and he's too close but he won't go.' At that moment there was a roar of exhaust and the bike and the leather-clad rider streaked past and disappeared. Tessa relaxed.

'I hate it when people do that. He could have gone ages ago. I can't think why he didn't.'

* * *

Still deep in conversation they did not notice that about half a mile on a motorbike and rider had stopped and were sitting almost concealed in a tree-shaded gateway watching as they drove past. Waiting until the car was almost out of sight, the rider slid cautiously onto the road again and followed.

Chapter 13

Reaching the house they were intercepted by Bunny.

'You know your ma's got a supper party on tonight?'

'Oh God, she hasn't. Who's coming?'

'I don't know. There's six of 'em is all she told me, and one of them's a veggie. I hate that. Separate this and separate that. It's a blinkin' pain.'

She turned away and stumped lopsidedly back into the kitchen. Following her in Tessa said, 'Make them all have the same.'

'I will not.' Bunny was affronted. 'I got my reputation to think of and, any case, your dad's home tonight and he won't thank me for veggie crap.' Tessa put an arm around her. 'I know perfectly well you'll turn out something so scrummy they'll all want to try it.'

'Hmph. D'you want some tea then?'

'Yes please. Is there any cake in the tin?'

'When isn't there cake in the tin, Miss? You fetch it out and I'll make the tea.'

Hester sat down at the kitchen table while Tessa wandered off to the pantry. After a moment she called out, 'Hester, come here.'

Reposing on the marble slab was a vast china pie dish with perfectly golden pastry covering it, decorated with exquisitely executed leaves and flowers and beside it a small dish in an exact copy. Tessa pointed to the small one. 'That'll be for "the veggie". And it'll be delicious. She's all talk you know.'

'What's in the big one?' said Hester with interest. Tessa bent down and sniffed delicately. 'Mixed game I'll bet, I'll see if she'll save us some.'

Hester was surprised. 'Aren't we in for supper?'

'No way. If it's the six I think it is they'll bore the pants off you. Besides someone's sure to recognise you, they've only got to put two and two together. No, we'll go out.

Tim's phoning later. We'll go to a nice quiet pub where no one will bother you.'

'Tim won't want me along,' Hester protested.

Tessa laughed. 'Don't be silly. I'm hardly going to leave you here, am I? Anyway he likes you a lot, he'll be happy to take us.'

'He's all right is Tim,' said a voice from the Aga. Bunny turned round waving a wooden spoon. 'He could have had his pick, could Tim, and he went and chose this one here.' Her expression softened as she looked at Tess. 'Used to upset you proper, didn't it, Miss? Coming home from college with all those long leggedy blonde bits and then one Christmas there you was, shining like a Christmas tree, and New Year you was engaged. Upset a few that did.' She gave a cackle of laughter and turned back to her cooking.

Amused Hester looked across at Tessa who sat stirring her tea, a faint flush on her brown cheeks. She looked up and grinned. 'I've been dotty about him since I can remember. I never thought I'd get him though. He never seemed to see me except as a sort of sister. Bunny's right. One gorgeous blonde after another every holidays and then one year, he came back on his own.' She smiled reminiscently. 'I'd had a few drinks and we all came back here on Christmas Eve, a great crowd of us and everyone was kissing everyone and I kissed him.' She stopped.

'And then?' Hester prompted.

Tessa hesitated. 'Fireworks. Unbelievable. For him too. We just stood there and kept kissing each other. He was shaking, I was shaking, and then he said… he said…' She stopped, cleared her throat. "All this time you were under my nose." That was it really. He went out and bought a ring and we got engaged in the New Year.'

'Great relief all round,' said a terse voice from the stove. 'Their parents couldn't think why it took them so long. Now everybody's happy.'

'That's right.' Tessa put the last piece of cake into her

mouth and licked her fingers. 'I'll go and phone Tim. He'll be at the surgery by now.'

She closed the kitchen door firmly behind her and picked up the phone in the hall. After a few minutes conversation she glanced towards the kitchen and lowered her voice.

'If Adrian starts poking around don't tell him anything. He spotted Hester today and you know what he's like. Don't let him know where we're going this evening; he'll probably turn up if you do. Someone was behind us on a bike like his on the way home. I don't know his reg number so I'm not sure it was him but I don't want Hester bothered.'

'Fine. He hasn't been in touch so far but I'm glad you warned me. See you later.'

* * *

Tim had hardly replaced the surgery phone before it rang again. His brother's voice said cheerfully, 'Hi, bro, how's it going?'

'OK, mate, OK. And you?'

'No worries, long time no see. D'you fancy a beer this evening.'

'As if! You've seen Tessa I gather. She's only up for a day or two so I'm taking her out.'

There was a small pause then, 'Right, of course. Er, she had a friend with her, good looking bird, why don't we make up a four?'

Tim smiled rather grimly into the phone. 'You don't miss a trick do you? Tessa thought you'd recognised her.'

There was a chuckle from the other end. 'You can't blame me for trying. Come on, Tim, give me a break; it would be a real scoop for me if I could get an interview. Nobody else has got near her. She can see it first, we won't print anything she's not happy with.'

'Like your Countryside Alliance story I suppose? It's going to be a very long time before Tessa's ma comes round to you after that.'

Adrian was wheedling. 'Of course it won't be like that. Those fanatics set themselves up. I can do sympathetic.'

'No.' Tim was uncompromising. 'She's up here for a break, to get away from sharks like you. Leave her alone.'

Adrian was sharp. 'I'm just a little minnow me. A tiny fish in a very small pond. You know I want to get to London and this could be a start. A good interview I can sell to one of the big boys. There's a lot of murky water around Hester Trent and I'd like the chance to stir it up a bit. After all, it only takes a word in the right ear and they'll all be down here like vultures. Looks like she's run away, doesn't it?'

Tim's voice was hard. 'You can really be a shit, Adrian. She has not run away. The ceiling has come down in the restaurant and she's had to close it for a few days so she's here on a bit of a holiday. So you give her a break. I'll talk to Tess and see if I can sort something out for later on but at the moment she won't talk to anyone. You'll just scare her off.'

There was silence at the other end and then Adrian said, 'Please yourself. I'll see you around' and the line went dead.

Tim sat silently for a few minutes, thinking. He knew his brother. Not for one minute did he believe that Adrian had given up but there wasn't a great deal he could do about it apart from warning Tessa. He looked at the clock and swivelled back to the computer. If he didn't finish soon they'd be too late to get a decent meal anywhere.

* * *

Dusk was beginning to fall as Hester and Tessa came out of the back door of the house and lights were coming on

135

in the stable cottages. As they got into the car Hester asked, 'How long have the stables been converted?'

'About five years,' Tessa answered swinging through the gate. 'Things have been pretty tough for farmers for a good while now, even for landowners. Regulations, red tape, European Union, Foot and Mouth. 'Diversify' says this government, they haven't got a bloody clue.' Tessa was derisive. 'Dad's sold off a fair bit of land. Home Farm's gone, sold to a London businessman with a blonde totty wife and two foul children. It's enough to make you weep.' She sounded quite savage.

'And the stables?' Hester prompted.

'Oh yes. Well, a friend of Dad's suggested it. He's the estate agent we went to this afternoon. Dad had the plans done and they were passed. He hasn't sold them all, only one, and the others are rented out. It's amazing what people will pay to live in a stable yard.'

'Reflected glory I imagine. Pretending to be to the manor born.'

'I suppose. Ma hated it. She said she didn't want a lot of strangers on the doorstep. She and Dad nearly fell out over it but when he showed her the figures she had to accept it. He started talking about having to sell the horses 'cos they cost too much and that shut her up. She hasn't got a clue really. It never occurs to her that everything can't go on as it always has.' Tessa sounded more indulgent than censorious and Hester thought momentarily of her relationship, or lack of one, with her own mother and felt a stab of sadness. To be part of such a solid, uncritical family must be such a firm base to build a future from. It was no wonder Tessa had such utter confidence in herself.

Glancing at the face beside her, serene under its shining cap of black hair, she thought again that Tessa looked almost out of place in this very English countryside. In the cosmopolitan mix of a tourist area, and the still visible influence of Spanish ancestry in some West Country families, it had not been noticeable before. This evening Tessa was in a geranium red linen dress scattered with huge black flowers with a barbaric bronze necklet and matching bracelets. She looked sleek and almost exotic.

'Tess, I hope you don't mind me asking but is there any Spanish blood in your family?'

Tessa laughed. 'Not Spanish, Italian. My mother's father was an Italian prisoner of war.'

Hester was astonished. 'How extraordinary! Do tell.'

Tessa turned off the main road into a narrow lane deep between high banks and slowed down almost to a crawl.

'Have to take this one slowly. Everyone round here drives like there's no one coming the other way and there's no room to pass except where they've cut into the banks.'

'Just like Devon. So go on.'

'Quite romantic really. My grandmother came from Somerset and they had several prisoners working in the farms down there during the war. Grandpa was very handsome and she was only eighteen. Of course all the young men had been called up and he didn't have any competition.' She pulled up in the shadow of the hedge to let an oncoming car get by and then continued. 'Big scandal. Grandma got pregnant with my mother. Apparently my great-grandmother was a complete autocrat and was determined she should have an abortion but great-grandfather supported her. She had the baby and Grandpa kept working on the farm and they lived in one of the tied cottages. After the war things were sorted out and they got married. Grandpa was a really hard worker and got on well with my great-grandfather and became farm manager.'

Hester was fascinated. 'It's very romantic. How did your great-grandmother cope with it all?'

'Oh, she came round in the end. When Grandma had a son to carry on with the estate she caved in completely.

Grandpa got to be more British than the British. Hunted, went shooting, fishing, the lot. He was a lovely, lovely man.'

'Is he dead?'

'Oh yes, about seven years ago. Grandma was completely devastated. She only lasted a couple of years afterwards. She just lost interest. She was the one who left me the money for the restaurant.'

'What a wonderful story. So if your mother lived in Somerset, how did she meet your father?'

'The usual thing. Her best friend at boarding school lived up here. She came to stay for a Hunt Ball, met Dad and that was it.'

'Another romance?'

'Definitely, though you wouldn't connect romance with them now.' Tessa was smiling as she negotiated a hairpin bend on to an ancient, narrow stone bridge. 'Ma drives Dad potty and they're always arguing.'

'They don't get on?'

'Of course they do. They're both strong characters and they wouldn't know what to do with someone who didn't fight back. Dad was pretty ill about two years ago and Ma was beside herself when she thought he wasn't going to make it. They're as solid as a rock and God help anyone who tried to hurt either of them. Right, here we are.' She pulled off the road onto a small car park, already almost full, in front of a long low black and white building bright with hanging baskets and tubs. 'The Fruiterer's Arms. You'll like it, great food and proper beer.'

Hester climbed out of the car and looked around.

'I thought you said a quiet place where no one will bother us. It's absolutely heaving!'

'Better a crowd to get lost in. What I meant was it's off the beaten track and not one of our regular haunts so we shan't have to introduce you to people. Tim and I go here when we want a quiet evening on our own.'

Neither of them noticed a motorbike parked under the trees on the other side of the bridge, the rider motionless, the helmeted face turned in their direction. As they disappeared inside, the motorcyclist rode slowly across the stream and slid into the car park stopping just inside the gate. He sat for some ten minutes before putting down the stand and walking cautiously into the side door leading to the lounge bar.

As Hester had predicted, inside it was heaving and the noise level was equivalent to a parrot cage in a zoo. Excusing their way towards the bar they caught sight of Tim's curly head and massive shoulders and at that moment he turned to look towards the door and saw them. He gestured towards the door marked 'Restaurant' and Tessa said, 'We'll go straight in, the table's booked.'

The restaurant was comparatively quiet after the cacophony outside and a pleasant-looking elderly woman came towards them smiling.

'Hi, Ida, Tim's booked hasn't he?'

'Table for three in the window and I've left a wine list on it. Tim said you're to choose, he doesn't know his Merlot from his Chardonnay.'

As they sat down Tim appeared with a tray and put it down on the table.

'Bloody Mary, one dry white and a beer. I hope I've got that right, Hester?' He bent down and kissed her cheek and she thought again, lucky, lucky Tess.

'How did you know I like Bloody Mary?' She said picking up the glass. 'From Devon when we went out. Remember?'

'Of course, thank you.' She lifted the glass, smiling at them over the rim.

'Here's to you two and thank you for coming to my rescue. I'm having the best time.'

The food was all Tessa had said it would be: excellent homemade duck paté followed by fillet steak grilled rare with a selection of mushrooms, Dauphinois potatoes and green beans cooked to crisp perfection. The women could not manage any pudding but Tim had no trouble coping with a mammoth helping of homemade treacle tart and custard.

Conversation ebbed and flowed as the level dropped in the bottle of Rioja that Tessa had chosen. Hester found herself talking far more easily than she had for years. It occurred to her that she was drinking most of the wine, the other two laughingly refusing more than a glass apiece.

'Can't afford to lose my licence,' Tim said as he refilled her glass a third time. 'A non-driving vet is pretty useless.' Hester felt so safe and comfortable with them that she relaxed completely. Tim asked her about the making of the television series and in talking of it Peter Armitage's name came into the conversation. Tessa remarked idly, 'He's the guy who got shot in Iraq, isn't he?' and in that second all the warm contentment drained away. Hester felt as if all the blood in her body had rushed to her feet and someone had encased her in ice. From a great distance she heard Tessa's voice.

'Hester, what on earth's the matter? You've gone as white as a sheet.'

She looked across the table at their concerned faces. They looked distorted and small, like reflections in a funfair mirror. For a few moments she couldn't speak, she was surrounded in a terrible silence and then she heard her own voice sounding thin and strange.

'Shot? When? How?'

'About ten days ago, I saw it on the television.'

'Why didn't I see it? How badly was he hurt? He's not...' She couldn't say the word, her throat closing against it.

'Dead? No, but badly hurt. He was in intensive care for a few days I think but I believe he's recovering now. Do you know him well, Hester?'

140

Hester laughed shakily, relief making her feel quite giddy. 'You could say that. But I don't understand why I didn't hear about it.'

Tessa sat back in her chair. 'It was while all the fuss was on over Simon's girl. You remember you were sick of seeing it so you stopped watching the news for a few days but I still had the little telly in the caravan and I saw it there.'

Tim was still looking worried. 'Are you sure you're all right? You're very pale.'

Hester took a gulp of wine. 'I'll be fine. It was just a shock.' She tried to speak more lightly. 'We became very good friends while I was doing the series and we keep in touch. I did wonder why I hadn't had some sort of message from him when all that stuff broke about Simon in the papers. Now I know.'

At that moment a tall figure stopped at the table. 'Hi, folks. Fancy seeing you here.'

Tessa stiffened and looked balefully up at her future brother-in-law. 'What a surprise, Adrian. Are you having dinner too?'

'No, no. Just a drink with some friends.' His glance rested on Hester's face and then shifted to Tim's. 'Aren't you going to introduce me, bro?'

'Hester, this is my brother Adrian. He's a journalist.' Tim sounded chill and dismissive but Adrian seemed sublimely unaware. He stretched out his hand.

'Delighted to meet you, Hester. Can I get you a drink?'

'No thanks, we're just about to leave,' Tim answered curtly. 'I'll get the bill,' and he raised a hand to the waitress.

Adrian dragged up a chair from the empty table next door placing it next to Hester. 'So are you staying long?' he asked pleasantly as he sat down.

She watched him warily, unsmiling. 'I don't know yet. It all depends.'

'On what?'

'On lots of things.' She bent to pick up her bag. 'I need to go to the Ladies, Tess. Where is it?'

'I'll come with you.' Tessa darted a furious glance at Adrian as she got up. She started to walk towards the door but Hester did not move. Tessa turned to her. 'Are you coming then?' But Hester seemed rooted to the spot, her face as pale as it had been a few minutes before. 'What is it?' Tessa asked sharply, 'What's the matter?'

Hester said in a shaky voice, 'That's Simon. In the bar. I'm sure it is.'

Tessa looked towards the bar. She saw the back of a fair-headed man moving away and then he was lost in the crowd. She looked back at Hester. 'Are you quite sure? That could have been anybody.'

Hester shook her head. 'I'm not absolutely sure but I could have sworn...'

Tessa took her arm. 'I think you're seeing things. Come on, we'll go to the loo. See you outside, Tim. Bye Adrian,' and they moved away.

* * *

Adrian had missed nothing of this exchange and turned to Tim. 'Simon? That's the stepson isn't it? The chap who was involved with the jumper?'

'For God's sake, Adrian, give it a rest,' Tim snapped. 'Leave the poor woman alone.'

'No chance, bro. This is my job, remember.' He pushed back his chair and was gone, threading his way through the bar, eyes searching for the fair head that had so bothered Hester. He emerged into the foyer as a tall figure pushed through the front door and was gone into the car park. He followed cautiously but when he got outside the figure had disappeared. Groups of people standing chatting or getting into their cars obscured his view and after a few minutes it was clear that he was not going to find him.

'Bugger, bugger, bugger,' he muttered. He stood irresolute for another minute and then, shrugging, went back into the pub.

'Adrian, come on, mate, it's your round,' came a shout from the bar and he had perforce to rejoin his friends. He saw Tim and the two women leave the restaurant without a glance in his direction and his frustration deepened. 'I damn well am going to get a story,' he thought as he watched them go, 'and perhaps I won't do sympathetic.'

* * *

In the car on the way home Hester was silent until Tessa said, 'Do you really think it was Simon you saw?'

'I don't know now,' Hester answered tiredly. 'Perhaps I imagined it. I must have done because he can't know I'm here.'

'I shouldn't think about it any more,' said Tessa comfortably. 'You'd just had a big shock over your friend and you were all upset. As you say he can't possibly know where you are.' Hester didn't answer and Tessa glanced curiously at her averted profile. She was dying to ask about the wounded war correspondent, Hester's reaction had been so extreme, but it was quite obvious that now was not the time.

Chapter 14

Hester had a bad night. Images of Peter, shadows of Simon, chased through her dreams. She woke for the umpteenth time in the very early morning soaked in sweat, the remnants of a dream still with her. She was being chased down a long winding lane by a fleet of ghostly bike riders menacing, terrifying in black and silver with huge faceless helmets and she was running, running on leaden legs, her breath sobbing in her throat. They were almost upon her, surrounding her as she turned a corner and there was Peter standing in her path. He stretched out an arm towards her but she saw with horror his other arm hung uselessly at his side covered in blood and there was a great gaping wound in his chest. She screamed and woke, heart thundering to the dim, quiet, safe room, grey light just creeping through a crack in the curtains. She lay still letting the relief wash over her and after a few minutes got up and went to the bathroom, sluicing her face with cold water and drinking a glass of it. Restless, she wandered over to the window and drew back the curtain. The parkland stretched in front of her, silent and still, shrouded in thin mist. She could only see as far as the first belt of trees and stood for several minutes absorbing the peace and beauty of it when a slight movement under the trees caught her gaze. Straining her eyes she could just make out a figure but it was too far away to see if it was a man or a woman. There was another movement and the figure melted away into the woodland and after watching intently for another few minutes Hester began to think she had imagined it. Trailing wearily back to bed she fell into a deep untroubled sleep woken by Tessa breezing in with a tea tray.

'Fancy a ride again? I thought we might go out early and have breakfast afterwards.'

Hester sighed. 'If you don't mind awfully I don't think I

will. I feel shattered this morning.'

'Bad night?' Tessa asked sympathetically as she handed her some tea.

'Rotten. Too much rich food and wine I expect. I don't normally drink a great deal as you know.'

'It'll do you no harm at all,' Tessa replied briskly getting off the bed. 'All work and no play you know.' She grinned as she went to the door. 'You need to get out more, sweetie.'

Hester smiled to herself, sipping her tea. There was probably more than a grain of truth in that. She lay back on the pillows thinking over the events of the previous evening. Her first thoughts were of Peter. Somehow she must find out how he was. Trawling her memory for possible contacts she decided her best chance was the producer of her programme who would not be surprised to receive a casual enquiry of friendly concern. The telephone number she needed was in her notebook at home so she decided to make her daily call to David as soon as possible and get him to find it. The problem of what to do about Simon she replaced firmly at the back of her mind except for an uncomfortable niggle as to whether her momentary sighting in the pub could possibly have been him. Deciding she was in danger of becoming obsessed on that subject she finished her tea and went to shower.

Later at breakfast she met Tessa's father, Alex, for the first time. He and Tessa came in together, both in jeans, padded waistcoats and stockinged feet, bringing the fresh air smell of early morning as they sat down at the kitchen table. He shook Hester's hand very firmly.

'Glad to have you with us, Hester. I hope my daughter's been looking after you.'

'Very well indeed, thank you,' she responded, surveying him with interest and liking what she saw. Tall and spare with the bony weathered face of a country man, sharp grey eyes under thinning pepper and salt hair and a humorous mouth which was smiling affectionately at Bunny as she put an enormous plate of bacon, eggs, sausage and fried bread in front of him.

'Get that down you,' the old woman said, her own mouth twitching into almost a smile. 'Ketchup?'

'Yes please,' he answered, squirting a generous dollop onto the plate. 'This should help keep me going all day.'

Bunny looked sharply at Tessa. 'What about you, Miss? Same as your dad?'

Tessa looked longingly at her father's heaped plate and sighed. 'I'd love it but better not. Just some brown toast please and fruit juice.'

'Hmm,' Bunny snorted, 'you and your friend, as bad as each other, watching your figures, load of rubbish. A good cooked breakfast never did anyone any harm.'

Tessa made a face at Bunny's outraged back. 'Change the record, Bun, you know perfectly well I put on weight at the drop of a hat.'

There was no answer and into the silence Tessa's father said, 'I'm going to Worcester today, girls, I've got some business. Do you want to come? I'll be there for the afternoon.'

Tessa looked at Hester. 'Do you fancy it?'

'Why not. I've never been. I believe the cathedral is very fine.'

'Oh it is. It's lovely and so are the shops. There are some good restaurants too, they're springing up like mushrooms.'

'Great!' Hester turned to Alex. 'I'd love to do that, thank you.'

Unselfconsciously he wiped the last of his egg up with a piece of bread and butter and popped it into his mouth. 'Excellent. I'll be ready at twelve o'clock. Thank you, Bunny, that was wonderful. Better than any London hotel. See you later, girls,' and he padded out, cup of tea in hand.

146

Bunny watched him go with the softened expression on her face that seemed to be reserved only for him and then turned back to Tessa.

'Are you two in or out this evening?'

Tessa looked at Hester. 'In, I think, unless you have other ideas?' Hester smiled at Bunny. 'Definitely in. I won't forget that steak and kidney pie in a hurry.'

Bunny gazed back with the merest hint of a smile. 'Have to see what I can do then' and she turned away to the sink.

'Is it OK if I ask Tim?' Tessa enquired.

'Don't make no difference, there'll be plenty.'

Finishing their breakfast they went out into the hall, Tessa smiling to herself.

'Tim is second only to Dad in Bunny's affections,' she said quietly, 'she really is a man's woman and men need feeding up in her book. Her husband was six foot four and built like Tim so he is her idea of a proper man.'

'And yours?' Hester enquired demurely.

'Most definitely,' Tessa replied with her own face softening. 'Anyway,' she continued briskly, 'I've got some phone calls to make and Ma needs a hand with the horses so I'll see you about half eleven, yes? We can have a coffee before we go.'

'Fine, I've got a couple of calls to make myself so I'll see you then.'

* * *

About this time Adrian was padding into his kitchen feeling, as he would put it, 'a bit shabby'. The previous evening had developed into quite a session and as it was not his turn to be the designated driver he had rather let himself go. 'Black coffee and then some solids I think,' he muttered turning on the kettle before opening the fridge which proved to be to all intents and purposes empty. A small mouldering lump of cheese, a scrap of butter in crumb-encrusted paper and half a lemon were the sum total of the contents apart from several bottles of wine in the door compartment.

'Bastard,' he groaned surveying the littered work surfaces with distaste, evidence of his flat mate having entertained friends with bacon and eggs and lager at the end of a presumably convivial evening. 'First stop the supermarket.'

Finding that there was barely enough coffee left to make a decently strong cup put him into an even worse temper and drove out any thoughts of the previous evening. He showered rapidly, dressed and left the flat, slamming the door behind him and riding off in a roar of exhaust.

Ten minutes later, wandering the aisles of the small local convenience store his attention sharpened and he stopped dead behind a pyramid of cereal packets. Bending over peering into a freezer cabinet was a tall fair-haired man in motorcycle leathers with a profile very familiar from recent newspaper photographs. The memory of Hester's pale, shocked face came immediately to Adrian's mind and he let out his breath in a silent whistle.

'Looks like it was you last night, sunshine. Have we a stalker here I wonder.' Adrian stayed motionless until the figure moved on and then, picking items at random from the shelves as he went, Adrian followed, ending up immediately behind the man in the queue at the till. Out in the car park he made his way quickly to his bike, stuffed the shopping into the bag strapped to the back and put on his helmet. A little further down the park he could see the man he knew to be Simon from the newspaper coverage doing the same. Cautiously allowing two cars between them he followed him out onto the road. Through the town he was able to tail him comfortably in the volume of traffic but as soon as they reached the outskirts the bike ahead took off at speed and although he snaked past two elderly motorists, hugging the crown of the road at considerable risk to oncoming traffic, he lost him. Cursing with exasperation he continued for a couple of miles but there was no sign of bike or rider. Dejectedly he started back, riding more slowly, looking into gateways and up drives hoping for a sighting. Almost at the edge of the town he glanced into the entrance to a large field with a sign saying 'Riverside Farm Caravan Park' and there was the bike, neatly parked by a large motorhome just inside the gate.

'Gotcha,' he breathed with satisfaction. Parking his own bike in the lee of the hedge he sauntered through the gate and past the motorhome, making for the back door of the farmhouse. A burly red-faced man in stained baggy corduroys opened the door and broke into a smile when he saw his visitor.

'Hello, young Adrian, what can I do for you? Lost dogs or pussies is it or have I got a mass murderer lurking in my park?' The jovial, patronising tone raised prickles of irritation but Adrian ignored them and managed an answering grin. 'I wish, Fred, I wish, it's too bloody quiet by half at the moment. I'm afraid I'm after something much less exciting. Can I come in?'

'Sure,' the farmer stood back. 'D'you want a cuppa tea?'

'Great,' Adrian replied stifling the longing for strong black coffee. 'I just want a few minutes of your time.' He sat down at the table while the old man put a large steaming mug of dark tan-coloured fluid in front of him and sat down opposite.

'Oh yes, what's it all about then?'

Adrian sipped the scalding liquid managing not to grimace. 'We're doing an article about the Government's advice to farmers on diversifying to survive and I'm trying to get some different views from people who've managed it and some that haven't. You've been very successful with

149

these caravans, haven't you, Fred?'

'Oh I wouldn't say successful. We're just about getting by,' the farmer said cautiously. Adrian hid a smile. Fred's meanness was legendary in the district but the success of his new venture was equally well known and had caused a good deal of envy in the less entrepreneurial neighbours.

'Well, can you give me an idea of how you got started, what made you decide to do it and so on? You know, just general stuff.'

It took a little while to get him going but gradually Adrian's skilful questions and the farmer's pride in his own farsightedness broke through his country-born suspicion and the interview went smoothly. He took Adrian outside to see the shower block he had built with two washing machines and dryers in a separate utility area, and talked of the plans he had submitted for a club room to be built adjoining the existing buildings. As they walked around, with Adrian pretending to take notes, he kept his eye on the motorhome and as they passed it he said casually, 'Nice one that, very smart. American style, isn't it?'

'Don't ask me, I don't know one sort from t'other. Tis a big 'un for sure, he can park that bike inside the back of it y'know, but I don't care what sort it is as long as they pays their fee, I don't care.'

'Do they have to pay up front?'

'Oh yes, cash only. I don't have no truck with plastic.' He heaved a gusty sigh. 'But I'll have to in the end, my accountant's not happy with all this cash. Trouble with the revenue, bloodsuckers that they are.'

'So is it mostly families you get here then?' Adrian asked, quickly steering Fred away from his favourite subject of the iniquities of tax inspectors.

'Summertime it is but we get lots of retired couples this time of year.' He pointed back at the motorhome. 'That one's just a young fella on his own. Very pleasant, says he's up here looking at properties to buy.'

Somehow I don't think so, thought Adrian, but out loud he said offhandedly, 'Staying long is he?'

'Don't know, he pays by the day.' Fred glanced at him sharply. 'You interested in him particular?'

'Not at all,' Adrian replied smoothly, adroitly changing the subject. 'So how long do you reckon it'll be before you can get the club up and running?' and with letting off steam about the difficulties of dealing with council planners and the wicked prices charged by plumbers and electricians, Fred's interest was averted. Half an hour later Adrian managed to extricate himself and as he left the farmhouse he saw to his fury that the bike had gone. Riding back into town he decided his best plan was to go into the office, call up on the computer all the information he could find about Simon, Hester and the cliff-jumping girlfriend and then talk to his editor. Prickles of anticipation ran up his spine as he went into the office building. This might just be the big one if only he could run with it.

Chapter 15

Driving into Worcester Tessa slid a sidelong look at her friend. Hester was gazing out of the window, her face carefully blank. She had given only monosyllabic replies to various remarks Tessa had made and Tessa felt quite sure something had occurred to upset her. She relapsed into silence until they had been dropped off opposite the cathedral, then she asked, 'What first? Do you want to have a look at the shops, cathedral or lunch?'

'I don't really mind.' Hester sounded distracted.

'Right, we'll do lunch first and then see. I know a super place, I'm sure you'll like it.' Hester made a very obvious effort to drag her mind back from wherever it was and was enthusiastic in her admiration for the beautiful Tudor buildings as they strolled up a narrow street to the restaurant, stopping several times to look in the enticing windows of the boutiques and jewellery shops jostling for space with the bars and restaurants of every nationality.

'I'd no idea Worcester was so... so... cosmopolitan,' she said as they turned away from looking at the menu board outside a Thai restaurant. 'I'm absolutely amazed.'

'I have to tell you that this is almost the best bit of Worcester,' Tessa said. 'Sadly the authorities destroyed a lot of the old city in the fifties and sixties. They tore down whole roads of Tudor and Victorian buildings and put up absolute monstrosities in their place, but apart from that awful car park this street is pretty untouched.' She stopped at a glass door under a brightly painted sign.

'Here we are, the owner is an old friend of mine and I'm sure he'll look after us,' and she was right. Enthusiastically greeted and hugged and Hester's hand warmly shaken they were soon settled at a secluded table with a well-chilled bottle of Sauvignon in an ice bucket between them. Having given their order, Hester clinked her glass to Tessa and leaning back heaved a sigh of pleasure.

'This is really delightful.' Hester looked around the restaurant. Softly lit and decorated in cheerful shades of ochre and saffron yellow it had the laid-back ambience of the sixties bistro. 'Fascinating,' she said looking at Tessa over the rim of her glass. 'It's really quite retro but obviously successful. You can always feel it, can't you?'

'Oh yes,' Tessa responded. 'It's one of the most successful in town. It's the second restaurant Bruno has run here and he's simply replicated the décor and people love it. As soon as you walk in you feel relaxed and comfortable and you just know you're going to be taken care of.' She hesitated and then said with a slight smile, 'So do you feel safe enough to tell me what's bothering you?'

Hester looked startled and then she laughed. 'You don't miss a trick do you? I didn't want to discuss it in front of your father but I am bothered. I rang home this morning and I spoke to Andy because David wasn't there.' She paused.

Tessa took a sip of wine. 'And?' She prompted.

'Well, they're getting on pretty well. The kitchen should be operational again by tomorrow evening. My shower isn't completed but I could sleep in the spare room for a couple of days and use the other bathroom and we could open again at the weekend. So we could go back the day after tomorrow. How do you feel about it?'

'Fine,' Tessa said firmly. 'No problem. But that all sounds very good, so what's upset you?'

'Andy mentioned that Simon was there a couple of days ago in a terrible temper, asking where I'd gone and David told him.'

Tessa drew a sharp breath. 'I see. So now you think that perhaps it was him you saw last night.'

Hester gazed unhappily back at her. 'Yes, and it's really thrown me. I mean, it seems positively deranged to follow me all the way up here. For what? Just to see what I'm

153

doing and who I'm with? It's bizarre.'

'Not just bizarre, it's sick,' said Tessa grimly. 'He's stalking you, that's what he's doing.' She sat silently for a few moments and then she ventured, 'It's as if he's taken a step across the line of acceptable behaviour, as if he's lost sight of normality now, and believes he's got a right to do whatever he likes as far as you're concerned. I don't like it, Hester.'

'Imagine how I feel.' Hester's voice rose and the couple at the next table looked curiously at her. Tessa laid her hand over Hester's clenched knuckle and gradually she relaxed. 'Perhaps I'm imagining the whole thing. It probably wasn't him at all and I'll find he's been at home all the time when I get back.' She looked hopefully at Tessa.

'Very probably,' Tessa was reassuring. 'It doesn't seem likely he'd have come up here when he's only got to wait for you to come back. After all, the business of that girl seems to have died down and there's been nothing else to set him off as far as we know.'

Again the memory of the softly closing bedroom door echoed faintly in Hester's mind but at that moment their food arrived and determinedly she banished the thought and settled down to enjoy it.

They sat for a long time over their lunch finishing the wine and then coffee. The owner came and sat with them for a while, obviously pleased to have Hester in his restaurant and interested to know her opinion of the food. She was able to say quite truthfully that it had been excellent and they spent some time discussing Tessa's new venture and the sort of menus she intended to use. Emerging into the sunshine Hester opted to go and look at the cathedral and when she saw that there was Evensong every day at four she said to Tessa she would quite like to stay and listen to Worcester's famous choir. Tessa wanted to do some shopping so they arranged to meet outside at five o'clock.

As she sat waiting for the service to start a smiling cleric came over and explained that the public could sit in the choir stalls for that service and ushered her up to the chancel. The small lamps were lit on the choir stalls and the stained glass windows shimmered with the colours from the late afternoon sun streaming through them. The organ was playing softly as the choir and clergy mounted the steps, robes and cassocks rustling against the stone. The music swelled, the wonderful treble voices soared and Hester felt her throat tighten and tears prick her eyes. At that moment she was transported back to her childhood, attending Bath Abbey with her father. The reassurance of continuity in the sonorous verses of the Nunc Dimittis and Magnificat, the rhythmic chanting of the psalms and glorious soaring chords from the organ swept her up and held her in a strangely familiar and comforting embrace.

She emerged into the late afternoon sunlight feeling as if her troubled mind had been washed smooth and clear and all her problems were no longer insurmountable. Tessa was waiting for her on a bench under the huge chestnut trees on the cathedral green and looked at her in astonishment. 'Something has certainly given you a lift, you look really happy.'

Hester laughed. 'That sounds as if I've been a proper misery but yes, it really did me good. Heaven knows, I'm not religious but that was thoroughly grounding. I'm so glad I went. It just reminds you that some things haven't changed and it's all there if you need it.'

Tessa looked slightly bewildered if relieved. She tucked her hand in Hester's arm and squeezed it gently. 'Good. As long as it's made you feel better. Come on, we'll cross over and wait by the car park for Dad to pick us up.'

* * *

From the shadows under the trees at the side of the cathedral a rider sat motionless on his bike watching the linked figures walking across the grass, the taller figure bent towards the smaller in a gesture clearly indicative of affectionate familiarity. His hands tightened on the handles until the knuckles turned white. In a furious jerky gesture he pulled on his leather gauntlets and started the engine. As he watched a car pulled up alongside the women and they got in. Circling the roundabout the bike fell in behind them, the rider's blue eyes like chips of ice staring ahead, intent on the two heads visible through the rear window.

* * *

Adrian was walking down the steps as Tim pulled up.

'Hi, bro,' Adrian shouted cheerfully. He waited for Tim to lock the car and then turned back to enter the house with him. 'I've just popped in to see the old man.'

'That's nice,' said Tim dryly. 'He's been asking about you. It must be at least three weeks since you've been.'

'Well, you know how it is,' Adrian responded airily, 'busy busy. Anyway how are things with you? Tessa not gone back yet?'

'Day after tomorrow apparently. Beer?' He opened the fridge door and took out two cans, handing one to his brother. Leaning on the kitchen table he watched Adrian's face with amusement. Annoyance was clearly visible. He took a mouthful of his beer. 'Sorry, mate, you won't be able to have a go at the lady chef. Bad luck.'

Adrian swallowed his irritation with an effort.

'Come on, bro, give me a break,' he wheedled. 'You could get me an interview. What's happening this evening? Why can't we meet up for a meal?'

'Because,' said Tim deliberately, 'I'm going to the Old Hall for supper and you can hardly expect to be invited there, can you.'

156

'Well, how about tomorrow?'

'No.' Tim finished his beer and unhitched himself from the corner of the table. 'She knows you're a journalist and she would just clam up. She's had a rough time, Adrian. She's a friend of Tessa's and I'm not going to help you chew her up even more. Now, are you going to see Dad? I've got to shower and change.'

'I've already seen him.' Adrian sounded like a thwarted child. 'You are a bugger, Tim, you could help me if you would. You know how I need a good story to get me a break.'

'Yes, I do,' said Tim evenly. 'If I could help you without hurting a friend I would do, but I can't and I won't so just give it up.' He looked at his watch. 'I'll have to get going or I'll be late. See you,' and he disappeared into the hall.

For a few minutes Adrian stood hesitating and then made for the door. There's more than one way to skin a cat, he thought as he started the bike. Let's see what Simon Brown is up to. He rode through the town and parked a few yards up the road on the opposite side from the caravan park. He was about to cross over when he heard a motorbike start up. Quickly remounting he waited and in a few moments the now familiar figure rode out of the gate towards the town. He followed cautiously keeping well back until he saw the rider turn into the car park of a well-known old pub in the centre and parked up at the far end. He followed his quarry as far as the reception desk where he waited out of sight while the bike helmet was deposited and, after doing the same, he strolled into the bar and snaked his way through the crowd of drinkers fetching up unobtrusively beside the tall figure in leather jacket and jeans. He waited until his neighbour had received his beer and turned away, slightly jogging his arm spilling his drink. Grabbing at some paper napkins stacked on the bar he tried ineffectually to dab at the wet patch on the man's jacket.

'Sorry, mate, sorry. Here, let me...'

The stranger brushed away his hand and he received such an icy glare from the blue eyes that he was momentarily stopped in his tracks. It was gone as soon as it had come and a perfectly pleasant voice said, 'Not your fault. Don't worry about it. It'll soon dry.'

Recovering, Adrian hurried into speech. 'No, really, I do apologise. Let me buy you another beer.'

'No need.' Dismissively the man turned back to the bar. 'Any room in the restaurant?' he asked the barman.

'Sorry, sir, we're fully booked but we serve in the bar if you can find a table free.'

Adrian said quickly, 'There's a couple just leaving at that one in the corner, you can get it if you're quick. I was hoping to eat, do you mind if I join you?'

'Of course,' was the colourless reply and very shortly they were seated at the corner table.

Their food ordered and drinks in front of them Adrian kept up a flow of practised commonplaces receiving the briefest of replies but gradually the chilly atmosphere eased a little and Adrian began cautiously to probe.

'Nice part of the world this, isn't it?' he started chattily. 'Lived here all my life, my dad's the local vet. You on holiday?'

'In a way,' was the careful reply.

'Adrian leaned back in his seat looking casually around him. In fact he was searching the crowd for acquaintances and praying no one would come breezing over and blow his cover.

'I used to know everyone around here but the place is growing so fast I can come in here and not see a soul. I see lots of new building going on these days. Not in the property line, are you?'

'Not exactly.' Silence fell and Adrian let it lengthen. With an effort his companion said, 'I am looking around. I recently sold a property and need to reinvest.'

'There are some great places on the market here at the moment.' Mentally crossing his fingers he continued, 'A lot of conversions, farm buildings and stable blocks. I believe there's one coming up for sale at our local manor house, Old Hall. They've done a grand job with those, kept all the old character.'

As if a switch had flipped he felt his companion's interest click in. 'Really? Where's that?'

'About a mile out of town. Lovely old place, a nice family. My brothers and I grew up with the kids. In fact my brother Tim is engaged to the daughter, Tessa. Lucky dog. Not that they seem to see that much of each other.'

'Oh, why's that?' The other man's eyes were now fixed on his face so intently that he began to feel uncomfortable. He picked up his glass and drained it.

'He's only just finished veterinary college and gone into partnership with my dad and she's been travelling all over the place. She's training as a chef and hoping to open her own place one day but she's been away all summer working in Devon with a TV celebrity chef. Hester something or other. Another beer?' He picked up the empty glasses.

'Yes, thanks.' Adrian could feel the cold blue eyes on his back all the way to the bar. An old rhyme came into his head as he stood waiting. 'I do not like thee Doctor Fell'. No I do not, he thought. The reason why I cannot tell but you are one spooky guy. Arranging his face into an expression of fatuous bonhomie he carried the drinks back to find his food had arrived. He had only picked up his knife and fork to begin when he was questioned.

'So does your brother expect his fiancé back soon?'

'Oh, she's here at the moment and brought her employer with her.' Adrian took a large mouthful to give himself time to think. Swallowing he said dismissively, 'Some building problem I believe. They had to close for a few days but they're due back shortly. Day after tomorrow

I think.' He was beginning to feel apprehensive that his interrogator would start to smell a rat at the way he was haemorrhaging so much information to a perfect stranger but it became obvious that he was far too intent on his own agenda. He did not seem aware that his food was untouched.

'So is she intending on staying on in Devon?'

'Lord, I don't know,' Adrian said carelessly. 'She and this woman seem to be bosom buddies so she may be there a while yet. No doubt she'll return eventually.'

'I see.' His companion got up abruptly. 'I'm sorry, I'm afraid I have to go. Nice talking to you.'

Startled, Adrian started to say, 'But you haven't even...' but he was gone, shouldering his way through the crowd. Adrian saw him pause briefly at the reception desk, pick up his helmet and walk out into the dark.

'Bloody hell.' Adrian gazed at his departing figure. 'Weird or what. Well, I'm going to finish this,' he said to himself picking up his knife and fork. 'If I'm going to be following him around God knows when I'll get any more. At least I know where to find him in the next half an hour or so.'

Chapter 16

Bunny had obviously decided that tonight she was really going to show what she could do.

'I've laid up in the dining room,' she barked at them when they trooped into the kitchen on their return. 'And you can leave that cake tin alone, Mr Alex. I want you with good appetites come dinnertime. I'll make you a cuppa tea but that's it.'

'Bunny, I'm starving,' said Alex plaintively, 'I've had nothing since breakfast.'

'You can have a couple of biscuits but that's your lot,' she said sharply, her tone belied by the twinkle in her eyes.

Having sat meekly in the sitting room drinking tea and eating what turned out to be delicious homemade Shrewsbury biscuits they all separated, Alex hopefully looking for his wife in her study and the girls to shower and change. Tessa said to Hester as they went upstairs, 'This is going to be good. You've really put her on her mettle. She's great when she's not really trying, so tonight should be something else.'

It was indeed. Sensing that it was expected Hester put on the only dressy frock she had brought with her, a flowing silk jersey dress in rich copper colour with a loose cowl neck and long sleeves. She clasped one of Peter's rare presents around her neck, a thickly twisted rope of varied brown and gold glass beads, with a matching bracelet, which he had brought her from an assignment in Venice. As she sat at the dressing table brushing her hair and twisting it into a complicated knot at the back of her head, the gold flecks glittered in the glass and she felt a fierce stab of longing. The memory of his fingers touching her skin as he fastened the clasp and then stood back to admire her was suddenly so painful that unconsciously she pressed her hand over her heart. The table lamp threw unkind shadows upwards onto her face and in that moment she was horribly aware of the fine lines around her eyes and the signs of slackening skin around her jaw.

'I'm getting old,' she thought. 'Four more years and I'm fifty and what have I got? A restaurant, friends I can count on one hand and...'

There was a tap on the door and Tessa came in.

'All ready?' she asked. 'Drinks in the library. Even Ma's making an effort tonight.'

Hester stood up snapping the tortoiseshell clip holding up her knot of hair and turning a smiling face to her friend.

'Will I do?'

'You look absolutely stunning,' Tessa replied, admiration plain from her expression. 'I shall have to keep Tim on a tight rein tonight and probably Dad as well.'

'You look pretty amazing yourself,' Hester said as they walked down the corridor. 'Brilliant colours really suit you, you've got such fantastic skin.'

'Legacy of my darling Italian grandfather.' Tessa swung ahead of her, the peacock silk of her skirt rustling against her legs, and opened the library door.

The picture they made as they walked in was enough to stop the conversation between Tim and Tessa's parents in its tracks. Tim gave a low whistle.

'Why didn't somebody tell me? I'd have put on the full rig. Girls, you look fabulous.'

'Hester my dear, come and sit over here, Alex will get you a drink. What will you have?'

Tessa's mother, resplendent in a rather too tight black velvet trouser suit, the effect slightly marred by a pair of stout brogues, drew her down on to the sofa beside her.

'Is that dry sherry you're drinking? I'd love one of those.' Hester smiled over at Alex who brought over the pale straw-coloured liquid in a delicately etched glass and handed it to her with a little bow. She sat back, listening to the easy banter interspersed with gentle teasing and family

162

references, and thought she had never met such kind and likeable people in her life. They had made her instantly welcome and totally at home with a complete lack of ceremony or pretension. She found herself fervently hoping that they liked her as much as she liked them and that she would be invited again.

As if in answer to her thoughts Tessa's mother, Ann, turned to her.

'Hester, we do hope this is only the first of many visits. Tessa has told us how much she has enjoyed being with you and what a lot she's learnt. You have been so generous with your time. I hope you'll be able to come up for her grand opening. Nothing like a TV celebrity to lend some glamour to the occasion.' She beamed hopefully at Hester.

Tessa broke in looking embarrassed. 'Mother, I haven't even mentioned it yet. You're jumping the gun as usual.'

'Of course I'll come,' Hester said warmly. 'I wouldn't miss it for the world. I can't believe we only met a few months ago. It's like I've known Tess for ever.'

Bunny's head appeared around the door.

'Come and get it,' she rasped and disappeared.

They entered the dining room and everyone exclaimed. It was lit only by candles: a huge eight-branched candelabra in the centre of the long table and four more double candlesticks on the sideboard and mantelpiece. Silver and mahogany gleamed, starched white napkins stood stiffly folded at each place and old cut glass caught the flickering light, shimmering with delicate rainbow colours.

'Well,' Tessa mother sounded completely astounded, 'I can't remember the last time we had all this.'

'Bunny darling, you must have been at it all day. It's marvellous.' Tessa put her arm around the old woman's shoulders.

'You'd best all sit down and get started or me soufflé'll drop.'

Bunny's sharp voice didn't alter but Hester, glancing at her as she sat down, caught the small satisfied smile as she turned to the sideboard.

The first course of cheese soufflé was a miracle of light, mouth-watering perfection. Tiny partridge exquisitely dressed accompanied by a green salad was followed by a carbonade of beef with crisp roast potatoes and garden vegetables. As she laid down her knife and fork Hester prayed that there wouldn't be a rich pudding because she knew she would never manage it, but after everyone begged for a pause and sat chatting and finishing their wine Bunny placed individual strawberry sorbet in front of them and left a cheese board on the table. Alex caught her arm as she turned to go.

'Bunny, sit down and have a glass of port with us.'

'Not tonight,' she answered pulling her hand away, 'we're doin' it proper tonight. I shall 'ave mine now, in the kitchen.' There was a burst of laughter from around the table and a reluctant grin dawned on her face. 'I'll take a glass with me though.'

Alex poured it with a flourish and as she took it from him he said, 'You have absolutely surpassed yourself tonight, Bunny. Here's to you, and thank you.' They all raised their glasses smiling and she stood for a moment looking at them all.

'So long as you've enjoyed it,' she said abruptly and turned again to go, but Hester caught the sheen of sudden tears. As Bunny reached the door, Hester said, 'If ever you want a change please come to Devon and teach me a thing or two. That was just the best.'

The old woman checked and half turned and then she was gone.

'Funny old love,' Tim said. 'She can't bear anyone to think she cares. I don't know who she thinks she's fooling.'

'Absolutely no one,' said Alex reaching for the port. 'Do you think you could come and stay on a regular basis,

Hester? We could do with a few more meals like that!'

'Greedy pig, Dad!' Tessa said smiling lovingly at him. 'You'd be the size of a house in no time.'

Much later as she and Hester climbed the stairs Tessa said casually, 'Did you manage to find out how your friend is?'

There was a small silence and then Hester said, 'Peter, you mean? Yes, I spoke to my producer. He's still in hospital over there but he's being brought back in a day or two.'

'Will you go and see him?' Tessa asked.

'Possibly. I'll keep in touch with the BBC and find out when he's home.' They had reached Hester's bedroom door and impulsively she bent forward and kissed Tessa's cheek. 'That was a wonderful evening. I haven't enjoyed myself so much for ages. I'm sure I'll sleep tonight.'

Tessa smiled her wide, curly smile. 'I hope you do. Goodnight.' She turned away and then over her shoulder she said, 'And just like Bunny, you don't fool me. "Possibly" indeed!'

Hester stood looking after her, bereft of words. As she went in and closed the door she started to laugh. Cleaning off her makeup she found she was smiling into the mirror. This was a real friend, the first since Fliss. Someone to whom she now realised she could say anything, someone she could trust and who would never judge. As she got into bed she decided that at some point she would tell Tessa about Peter and get her reaction. She had a slightly uncomfortable feeling that Tessa would tell her to stop putting her life on hold and take a chance on something else. Frank? No, definitely not. That chapter was closed.

* * *

Riding back to the caravan park, Adrian saw the motorhome nosing its way out through the gate.

165

'Now where's he off to?' he thought, driving straight past and turning in a driveway further up the road. The big van headed towards the town and drove sedately through it taking the turn on the last roundabout that led to the motorway. Following at a discreet distance Adrian mentally juggled with various possibilities. Was Simon on his way back to Devon or was he simply moving to another venue? If he was going home would following him be the best option or would trying to have another stab at getting an interview with Hester be more useful? As he mulled it over the van ahead took the junction for the M5 and settled into the slow lane at a steady sixty miles per hour. He followed for a short distance still trying to make up his mind and as the first junction came up he decided and came off, circling the roundabout and setting off back the way he had come. It looked very much as if Simon was homeward bound and if that was the case rather more preparation was needed. Adrian had on only light jeans and a shirt under his leather jacket and nothing else with him. Also, as he snaked from lane to lane at around ninety he debated as to whether it would be more sensible to use his car, which would give him a base from which to operate. The other side of the coin was that Simon had seen his face and in a motorcycle helmet he was more anonymous and the bike had more mobility.

By the time he pulled up at his flat he had made up his mind. The bike would be the best option, quicker, anonymous and more flexible. He changed quickly into full leathers, stuffing spare jeans, shoes, toiletries and an extra sweater into his bag. Quietly cursing that he didn't have a thermos or the necessary makings for a sandwich, he decided to stop at a services once he had located the van again and stock up with some supplies. It would not be a good policy to sit behind Simon at under the speed limit. He might well begin to notice a bike behaving in such an uncharacteristic manner.

166

He caught up with Simon just beyond Bristol and proceeded to play 'Box and Cox', streaking past and then slowing down after a couple of junctions, until the van came in sight again. Once on the A38 beyond Exeter he settled down well back to watch. When he had stopped at the services, after one of his bursts of speed, he had purchased a map of the South West and having checked the approximate area that he supposed the restaurant to be in he was uncertain which turn off Simon would take. Once in the narrow winding roads of South Devon he was able to keep far enough behind to avoid notice by simply following the headlights of the van in front. It was by now well past midnight and fully dark with no moon and heavy cloud cover. There was very little traffic, just the occasional car coming the other way, making it easy to follow. Through silent villages, the roads narrow and deep between high banks, becoming steeper as they made towards the coast, they eventually came out to the main Plymouth road turning left for a short distance and then right again onto a lane, narrower still. Concerned that Simon might become alert to his shadow, Adrian dropped back as far as he dared and after a few miles saw the lights ahead swing sharply round and come to a halt. He pulled up and waited and the lights died.

Switching off his own lights and killing the engine he pushed up his visor, removing his helmet and listening intently. Faintly, through the soft breath of the wind he could hear the distant hiss of surf and smell the hint of salt. The lane sloped very steeply ahead of him and clipping his helmet to the bike he freewheeled slowly without lights, following the lane downwards until he saw, just ahead of him, the white bulk of the motorhome parked inside a gateway. He pulled up silently and pushed the bike onto the verge, narrowly avoiding the deep concealed ditch beneath the hedge and, keeping well down, he crept along until he could see into the field.

The motorhome was parked in front of a car turned into the hedge. Craning around the corner Adrian recognised the lean lines of a Porsche and whistled silently. No shortage of money here, then. The lights were on inside the van but the curtains were drawn and he could hear nothing. Withdrawing cautiously he returned to the bike and sat on it, pondering. He was stiff and cramped from the long ride, and the possibility of a hot shower and comfortable bed were very seductive, but the only place he could hope to find at this time of night was at least three quarters of an hour away at a Travel Lodge on the A38 and the last thing he felt like was more travelling. A drink and a sandwich he thought and then perhaps he could make a decision. Having followed his quarry this far he felt curiously reluctant just to go tamely away and as he munched on his sandwich he realised just how odd all this was. It could only be a matter of a few miles to Hester's place so why was Simon camping out in a field? Still undecided on his next move he was stowing the empty can and sandwich wrappings back into his bag when he heard the bike start up in the field. Transfixed with surprise he only had time for the fleeting hope that Simon would not turn right out of the gate, because he had no hope of concealment, when the bike roared out and turned left. Breathing a sigh of relief he watch the lights as they swung in wide arcs negotiating the bends in the steep lane and then steadied as Simon obviously took a left turning and then disappeared below Adrian's line of vision.

He started up quickly and followed the direction Simon had taken keeping his own lights off. The left turning came up quickly with a small finger sign saying, 'Mackerel Cove, access only' and a road sign showing it was a dead end. Adrian slowed down and switched off the engine. He could hear, very faintly, the diminishing sound of Simon's engine and after another minute or two it ceased. Cautiously, braking frequently, Adrian freewheeled down the lane which became ever narrower and prayed that Simon would not, for whatever reason, turn around and come back but the silence remained complete. The clouds had broken and were scudding fitfully across a hazy moon which gave just enough glimmer to see where he was going. With almost no warning the lane broadened and levelled out and he was on short scrubby grass scattered with coarse sandy patches. He halted abruptly, straining his eyes. As they became accustomed he could see he was on a small plateau on the edge of cliffs, beyond which was the dull shimmer of the sea.

Turning his head cautiously he could see that the other bike was parked within about fifty yards of him but of Simon there was no sign.

Ten minutes passed and nothing stirred. Moving out a little way from the sheltering hedge Adrian looked around carefully. As far as he could tell there was no one on the cliff top with him but the prospect of covering the open space in front of him with no clear knowledge of Simon's whereabouts made him distinctly uneasy.

He waited another ten minutes and then having pushed his bike deep into a patch of bushes well away from the other one he grasped his heavy torch and glancing from side to side walked as fast as he could towards the cliff edge. No shout or running feet came after him and the prickling apprehension gradually subsided. He peered over the edge and could see below him a precipitous path winding its way down to the beach. The fitful moonlight made it impossible to see clearly but it seemed obvious that Simon must be down there. But doing what?

Well, Adrian thought, if what is happening on that beach is what this journey has been all about there's not much point in staying up here. He looked doubtfully at the path which, apart from being extremely steep, seemed to be scattered with loose shale and would be very difficult to cover without making a noise. With the feeling of someone stepping off a bank into an unknown depth of water Adrian set off. The broken surface of the path crunched under his feet every now and then and some pebbles would roll away sounding like the rapping of a machine gun to his nervous ears. On each occasion he stopped and listened but the soughing of the wind and the increasing noise of the waves below were all he could hear and no angry figure appeared demanding to know what he was doing.

With increasing caution he approached the end of the path and stepped on to the sand. From the deep shadow under the overhang he surveyed the tiny cove but there was no movement and no sign of any other person. On the horizon the sky was lightening and glancing at the luminous dial of his watch he saw that it was already close to dawn. From the corner of his eye he caught a movement at the far side of the beach and from the dense shadows a figure materialised. He could not see who it was because it appeared to be completely clad in close-fitting black, including a head covering, but from the height and build he assumed it to be Simon. He shrank back as far as he could against the rock face, his heart thudding with anticipation. Something very odd was going on, his instinct to follow had been absolutely right.

The figure walked awkwardly to the water's edge and Adrian realised it was wearing fins, goggles and snorkel. He felt a sinking disappointment. Perhaps this was just a diving exercise after all. However the figure did not move. It just stood motionless as if waiting for something, and then around the headland slid the unmistakable silhouette of a small fishing boat. The figure in front of him dropped behind a rock and the boat continued chugging diagonally across the bay. Adrian watched as it reached the opposite promontory where it stopped. It was too far away for him to see what was happening but suddenly he became aware of a small black object cleaving through the water and realised it was the diver's head as he swam steadily in the direction of the distant boat. Then, as it became too small to distinguish it disappeared completely. Adrian was conscious of intense frustration.

Instinctively he knew that he should be out there not stuck on dry land but there was nothing he could do, so he simply watched and waited.

A full hour later his straining eyes detected the small black object travelling back across the waves. He had moved further away from the path to avoid detection and was ensconced in the entrance to a small shallow cave further along the cliff. It was by now half light and as the figure waded out of the surf and pulled off goggles and snorkel, loosening the head covering, he could tell that it was indeed Simon. From his hiding place he watched the other man remove the fins and sit down on a rock to put on trainers. Carrying the gear he walked up the beach and disappeared up the cliff path. In the increasing light Adrian looked towards the fishing boat but could see no one moving on it and continued to wonder, as he had for the past hour, just what he had seen or not seen. He felt certain that Simon's behaviour was connected with the arrival of the boat but he couldn't work out in what way. He decided to wait for at least half an hour to make sure Simon had gone and prayed that his own bike would not be spotted. However when he finally emerged on the plateau his bike was still in its hiding place but the other one had gone.

Suddenly feeling intensely weary he rode back, passing the motorhome, but barely glancing at it he did not even notice that although the bike was there the car had gone. At the Travel Lodge he booked in and, too tired even to make a drink, fell into bed and was asleep immediately.

Chapter 17

In Herefordshire, Hester was having a gentle day. She had gone riding early with Tessa and helped to untack and rub down the horses. The atmosphere round Bunny had definitely thawed and while Tessa spent some time with her mother Hester sat at the kitchen table drinking coffee and carefully drawing Bunny out. Her genuine interest in how Bunny had started cooking and her own very different experiences led to some serious discussion and lively differences of opinion.

'I really envy you, Bunny,' she said at one point. 'You were so lucky having your mother-in-law to hand on all that knowledge and skill. My mother was useless in the kitchen, everything came out of tins and packets.'

'I expect that's what set you off then,' Bunny replied sagely. 'Deciding you didn't want to eat that sort of crap for the rest of your life.'

'Quite possibly,' said Hester, amused. 'I had to do a lot of entertaining when I first went up to London and I didn't know where to start so I enrolled on a cookery course, then I found I loved doing it for its own sake so I went on learning.'

'Done you all right then, hasn't it,' Bunny eyed her speculatively, 'must be worth a bob or two, your own restaurant and the telly shows and all.'

Hester laughed. 'I'm not complaining, I know I've been very lucky.'

'Yes, well, you make your own luck mostly I reckon. You just need one decent break and the rest is up to you. My break was being evacuated here, my luck was marrying my Martin.' She flashed Hester an impish grin. 'Mind you, God help any other girl who tried to get near him. Once I'd made me mind up he didn't stand a chance.'

'Tell me about him and his family,' Hester urged and, over another pot of coffee with elbows on the table and the softest expression Hester had yet seen, Bunny did. Hester listened, silent and fascinated to an account of a totally different way of life to anything she had ever been involved in, enhanced by Bunny's pithy and uncomfortably accurate descriptions of various village characters and her particular brand of mordant humour. When Tessa came in at lunchtime she stopped at the kitchen door in amazement at the two figures rocking with laughter at the table.

'What's going on?' she demanded. 'You two sound as if you're having a party! Can anyone join in?'

Hester ran her forefinger under her eyes. 'She's made me cry I've laughed so much. I've had a fantastic morning.'

Bunny got up abruptly. 'Right, get out of it, you two, I've got work to do. Will a sandwich do you now? I've got a nice leg of lamb for this evening.'

'Sandwich will be fine,' Tessa said. 'I'll do it, you get on with your other things.'

They took their lunch into the sitting room where the inevitable log fire smouldered. As they sat down Hester asked, 'Do you always have fires burning? I mean it's not cold.'

'Not in really hot weather.' Tessa took a generous bite of her sandwich. 'But this is a cold house and because the ceilings are so high it never gets warm in here and by evening it's pretty chilly.'

Taking the last bit of her sandwich she looked almost shyly at Hester. 'Would you be OK on your own this afternoon? Tim can take some time off and as we're leaving tomorrow…'

Hester interrupted her, smiling. 'Don't be silly. Of course I'll be fine. Off you go. I'll see you later.'

After Tessa had gone Hester put another log on the fire and sat back on the sofa, feet curled under her, watching the flames lick up around the new wood. The only sound in the room was the soft hiss of the fire and the gentle rhythmic ticking of the clock on the mantelpiece. She thought idly that this was the most relaxing few days she had spent for years and it was more than time that she started taking more regular breaks and gave herself permission to be lazy now and again. With a small shock she realised that she was actually not much looking forward to going back to work and that this was the first time she had not been anxious to return when she had been away. Time for some re-evaluation she said, half aloud, eyes fixed on the flickering flames and drifted effortlessly into sleep to be woken some two hours later with Bunny rattling cups on a tea tray.

Dinner that evening was a very relaxed affair. Tim and Tessa arrived smiling sleepily and exuding a sort of satisfied warmth that pointed to an afternoon most definitely spent indoors and exclusively together. The parents were out to dinner at a neighbour's house so they ate around the kitchen table, Bunny sitting down with them. Conversation centred around Tessa and Tim's plans for the new restaurant, changes to be made to the house and surgery and their wedding early in the New Year. Hester went early to bed leaving the other two curled up by the fire and slept again dreamlessly until Tessa woke her with morning tea. They planned to be away early but as they sat drinking the phone rang faintly downstairs and Tessa went off to answer it.

* * *

Adrian awoke much later than he had intended, having slept the sleep of complete exhaustion. He showered quickly, ate a hurried breakfast in the restaurant attached to the motel and rode back at speed to the field he had left in the small hours. To his disappointment the van was obviously unoccupied and the car was gone. The bike was nowhere to be seen either but he thought perhaps it was

174

inside the van to protect it from theft though that probability was pretty unlikely in such an uninhabited stretch of country. He sat for some minutes pondering and then got out his local map and scrutinised it carefully. There was the village two miles from Hester's restaurant which should be easy to find so that had better be his next port of call. Arriving in the village he was pleased to see there was still a local post office cum stores and received exact, if slightly difficult to follow, directions from the broadly-spoken Devonian behind the counter. There also seemed to be some drama attached to his destination and a lot of head shaking and doom laden remarks such as 'If 't'isn't one thing after another' and 'Talk about never rains but it pours', also 'Likely they won't let you near', which whetted his appetite and he got away as fast as he could. As he turned the corner into the lane up to the restaurant he could see the open area in front of the building very much occupied by two fire engines, a police car and several other cars including the Porsche. He pulled up, parked the bike behind a tree and made his way cautiously towards the scene.

At first he could not see any evidence of fire but edging his way unobtrusively around the perimeter he came to the side of the building and there in front of him were the still-smouldering remains of a caravan. A voice behind him said, 'Excuse me, mate, but you can't stay there, no public allowed,' and he turned to find a burly fireman towering over him. He took his card from his breast pocket and handed it to him. 'Press, just taking a look for my report.'

The fireman inspected it impassively. 'Hereford Journal, is it? You're a bit out of your area, aren't you?'

'On holiday down here,' was Adrian's glib rely. 'Heard about this in the village shop so I thought I'd take a look. Any idea what started it?'

The fireman handed back the card. 'You'd best talk to the police sergeant, not that they'll likely tell you anything.

Too soon to tell much.'

He stood back to let Adrian pass him and was obviously going to stay firmly behind him until he'd reached the policeman when a colleague shouted and beckoned him and he turned away saying with a jerk of his head, 'Sergeant Jarvis over there. Speak to him,' and lumbered off. Taking a quick look around him, Adrian whipped his tiny camera out of his jacket pocket and took three rapid pictures and then with the ease of long practice he snaked his way between the crowd of firemen, equipment and other assorted bodies and arrived quietly at the side of the police sergeant who was deep in conversation with another policeman.

'We'll have to wait for the forensics before we can get any further,' he was saying. 'At least we know there was definitely nobody in there. Bloody good job Brown was sleeping in the house and heard the noise and smelt the smoke. If that fire had caught the trees it could have spread to the house and then...'

He stopped, suddenly aware of Adrian's silent presence and turned abruptly.

'Who are you and what do you want?'

Adrian flashed the card again with a friendly grin. 'Press, just nosy press, Sergeant. On holiday here and heard about this. Couldn't resist coming to take a look.'

The sergeant looked him up and down disapprovingly.

'Well you've been and you've seen and now you'd better go. You'll just get in the way.'

'Just give me a little bit,' Adrian persisted. 'Vandals was it, or someone with a grudge or just an accident? You must have some theory.'

'Far too soon for that,' the policeman replied tersely. 'The fire's not even properly out. We'll be issuing a statement later. Now hop it,' and he started walking towards the caravan.

It was obvious that he was not going to get any further

for the present, so Adrian went thoughtfully away. In the distance he could see Simon's fair head bent to speak to someone and having no wish to take the chance of being recognised he skirted the crowd and picking up his bike from its concealment he rode slowly back to the village.

Sitting in the local pub, nursing a pint of shandy, he listened to the conversation eddying around him. The talk was all of the fire with a great deal of supposition and theorising and not much fact. The greatest body of opinion was that it was just another in a string of similar incidents considered to be the work of local disaffected young yobs. A hay barn had been set alight, a local stables had suffered, stock had been let out on to the road causing quite a serious car accident and so on. Everybody seemed to be quite sure who the culprits were but it seemed the police could not get the necessary evidence to charge them. There was a good deal of 'What they need is a bloody good thrashing' and 'If I caught my lad doing anything like that his life wouldn't be worth living', etcetera.

Adrian bought himself a cheese ploughman's and another half pint and continued to sit mouse-like in the corner of a deep, winged wooden settle while he thought over what he knew and considered what to do next.

The most intriguing thing from his point of view was the discrepancy between what he knew of Simon's movements the previous night and the police assumption that he had been peacefully asleep when the fire broke out.

It had been around four thirty am when he had left the field so if Simon had set off again immediately after that it was going to be around five to five thirty when he reached the house. Was the fire already raging when he got there and he'd lied about being asleep? Had he gone straight to bed and the fire broken out shortly afterwards? Or, for some reason that Adrian had not yet fathomed, had he started it himself? He realised that there was simply not

177

enough in an inexplicable late night swimming expedition and a small caravan fire to justify his staying in Devon any longer. If he wasn't careful his editor would start issuing dark warnings about time wasting and unjustified expenses so the best thing he could do was get back home, lay the whole thing in front of him and await further developments. The police statement would be unlikely to shed much light and it would be cursory at best but it would be useful to know at what time they judged the fire to have started.

Finishing his lunch he went outside and made a brief call on his mobile, wincing slightly and holding it away from his ear to distance the angry voice at the other end, and started on the long ride back.

* * *

Back in Herefordshire, Hester put down the phone with extreme care and looked at Tessa.

'I can see it's bad news,' Tessa said watching Hester's set face. 'What's happened exactly?'

'The caravan's been set on fire and it's completely burnt out.'

Tessa was horrified. 'Good God, how?'

'They don't know, yet. A forensic team is coming to investigate and the whole place is apparently awash with firemen and policemen and heaven knows who. I'll have to get back straight away.'

'Of course. Who was that on the phone?'

'David. Andy went up as usual at eight o'clock to find all hell let loose and he called David.'

'We'd better get our skates on. I'm all packed. How about you?'

'Yes I'm ready but I don't think we can both go.'

'Why not?' Tessa demanded.

'My shower is still not quite finished so the bedroom is

not fit to sleep in yet, which means there's only the spare room and nowhere for you to sleep.'

'Doesn't matter, I'll kip down on the sofa.'

Hester managed to smile at her. 'You are a brick but really there's no need for you to come today. We've got the two cars, thank goodness, so going separately is not a problem. I'll go down today and phone you later. As soon as my room is finished you can follow on. Obviously you can have the spare room and we'll put off opening the restaurant until next week.'

'If you're sure,' Tessa said doubtfully. 'I don't think you should be facing all this on your own. I'd rather be there.'

'Honestly, I'll be fine. There's David and Andy and I'll obviously have to talk to the police. Don't worry. I'll keep in touch.'

'Well. I can't force you to let me come but you will keep in touch won't you? Keep you're mobile on, you're a devil for having it switched off.'

Hester sketched another smile. 'I promise. Now, I'd better get moving.'

As Hester switched on the car engine Tessa leant into the open window. 'Who reported the fire?' she demanded.

'Oh, Simon apparently. He was sleeping in the house and woke up to hear the noise and saw the glow. David said it was just as well he was there otherwise it could have reached the house, the trees and scrub are so dry.'

Hester let in the clutch but Tessa stretched in and held her shoulder. 'Hester, I don't like this. Please let me come.'

'Now you're being silly. What on earth would be the point of Simon setting fire to the caravan? Sweetie, I've got to go. See you tomorrow or if not the day after.'

* * *

The car moved forward and Tessa perforce had to let go. She stood watching as it disappeared down the drive and then walked back into the house frowning. One good reason for setting fire to the caravan, she thought. To make pretty sure I can't come back today with only one usable bedroom between the two of us. And what's he doing using the house when she's not there? I don't like any of this.

As she crossed the hall Bunny came out of the kitchen.

'She's gone then? What are you looking so worried about? She doesn't need a nanny you know, she can look after herself.'

Tessa stared at her for a long moment. 'I'm not so sure.' She hesitated and then seemed to make up her mind. 'Make us a pot of tea. I want to tell you what's been going on and see what you make of it all. I've been too close to it, you'll probably tell me I'm making a mountain out of a very small molehill.'

But an hour later she sat back in her chair watching Bunny's face as the silence lengthened. Bunny stared at the dregs of tea in her cup and then, putting it down gently, looked up at Tessa.

'Pretty damn big molehill if you ask me, but not a lot you can do about it. It's all between the two of them and she's got to bring it out in the open and get it sorted. It'll just go on festering away until she does and one way or another he's got to be put straight.'

'But you do see why I'm so worried,' Tessa persisted. 'Some of the time he's positively unhinged.'

'Oh yes, I can see that, but I still say it's her business to sort out. All you can do is be there for her when she needs you.'

'Which is now,' Tessa said fretfully. 'I think I shall go down tomorrow, whatever.'

'You'll do what you'll do. You always have. Obstinate as a pig, since you were tiny.' She levered herself up holding the table and stood looking at Tessa with a flicker of a smile. 'I reckon young Tim won't know what's hit him once you're married. Get on with you now, I've got work to do.'

Chapter 18

Hester stood silently gazing at the charred carcass of the caravan, David at her shoulder.

'Rotten business on top of everything else,' he said presently. 'At least Tessa wasn't sleeping in there. It would have been a real tragedy.'

Hester sighed. 'I do realise that. It does just seem as if someone up there doesn't like me at the moment.'

David hesitated. 'You know you don't have to stay here tonight, Hester. I've spoken to Amy and you'd be most welcome to stay with us until your room is ready. Andy's working on it now and he reckons it will be finished tomorrow.'

Hester felt a small internal giggle rising up, instantly suppressed. She could imagine how chilly Amy's welcome would be.

'That's so kind of you both but I am perfectly well able to sleep in the spare room tonight. Simon can rough it in the gallery. As soon as Andy's finished Tessa will be coming down and we can re-open the restaurant. Please don't worry, I'll be fine. Now, I'll have to get on. I've got an interview at the police station at four o'clock and I want to have a good look at everything before then and talk to Andy.' She reached up and kissed his cheek. 'Bless you, David, you've been a good friend. I'm very grateful.'

He smiled down at her with a warmth that would have infuriated Amy. 'You know nothing is too much trouble as far as you're concerned. I'll see you tomorrow.'

She turned towards the house, smiling to herself. Why are all the nicest men so often married to ghastly women? she thought, and felt the comforting glow evaporate as the side door opened and Simon appeared. He strode across the grass towards her and started to lift his arms but as he reached her something in her face must have alerted him and he dropped them abruptly.

'So,' Hester said sharply, 'what exactly happened here last night?'

He stared at her, his face quite blank. 'You sound almost accusing. What's the problem? If I hadn't been here you could have lost the restaurant as well.'

Something in his voice, a hectoring almost bullying note, hardened her feeling of something not quite right.

'I realise that,' she answered deliberately calming her manner, 'as you say, I could have lost the whole thing but I'd still like you to take me through it. After all you haven't been around for a while and I didn't know where you were. I certainly didn't expect you to be here while I wasn't.'

He dropped his gaze and turned to the ruin of the caravan.

'I got back here about two o'clock this morning and went straight to bed. I was pretty tired so I was probably sleeping heavily. I didn't realise there was anything wrong 'til I woke up and needed a pee. It was when I was in there I smelt the smoke and realised that the glow outside wasn't daylight and then I heard the crackling. I saw something was on fire but I wasn't sure what so I went downstairs pretty quick. It might have started inside the house. Anyway I went outside and there it was, well ablaze. So I phoned 999 and then got the garden hose on it until they came. That's all really.'

Hester contemplated the burnt out wreck and could see where the lower branches of the overhanging tree were smoke-blackened and slightly charred.

'As you say, lucky you were here,' she said neutrally. 'So where have you been and why did you come back here last night?'

'Well, I thought I'd get back to meet you,' he replied easily. 'Now the repairs are pretty well completed I imagine you will be re-opening the restaurant and I can make myself useful.' He paused and then added, 'On your own? You haven't brought Tessa with you?'

'She'll be coming tomorrow, provided my bedroom is habitable. She can sleep in the spare room 'til the end of the season and she'll stay on as long as I need her.'

Silence. Then Simon said very quietly, 'I see. I thought you didn't like having anyone in the flat with you. Except me that is.'

She turned to face him. 'I don't. Not anyone except on a very temporary basis but Tessa has shown herself to be a good friend and I have become very fond of her. It'll be no problem.'

She turned away and started to walk towards the house but not before she had seen a flash of something in his face, which jolted her uncomfortably.

He fell into step beside her and said in quite his normal manner, 'I'd better shift my stuff back into the gallery then. I'll do it now.'

'That's another thing we have to sort out, Simon, but not now. I need to deal with all this mess first.'

'Of course, there's no rush. I've already spoken to David about drawing up plans but he said we'll have to apply for planning permission before we can do anything. I can't think there'll be any problem. After all it was a dwelling originally. Anyway, as you say, that's not for now. We can discuss it all later.'

They had reached the house and as he unlatched the door and stood back for her she opened her mouth to speak and then shut it again. He gave her a bright, empty smile and went off up the stairs two at a time and she turned into the restaurant feeling profoundly disquieted. It was as if nothing she had said had had any effect and he was oblivious to anything but his own internal agenda.

She went into the kitchen and was standing looking at the newly completed ceiling when the niggle at the back of her mind suddenly cleared. How had he known she was coming back today? Guesswork, or had he been in touch with David? She felt suddenly very vulnerable and wished fiercely that Tessa was with her and then mentally shook herself. Rampant paranoia or what! I'm being absolutely pathetic, she thought, and having thoroughly inspected the kitchen, which looked pretty well ready for use, she went upstairs. Andy was inside her shower working on the tiling and stepped out as he heard her come in.

'Hi,' he said, his usual grin splitting his dusty face. 'Nearly done. We'll be finished this afternoon but don't use the shower for another twenty four hours. I'll sweep up but you'll need to give the place a good clean. We've made a lot of dust. Can't be helped.'

She smiled warmly back at him, his cheerful normality calming her nervous discomfort.

'Thanks, Andy, it all looks fine. I'll use the spare room and shower tonight and get this cleaned up tomorrow. I'll leave you to it. I have to go into town to do some shopping, go to the bank and so on. See you soon.'

'OK.' He sketched a mock salute and disappeared inside the shower cubicle. As Hester came out of the bedroom Simon appeared in the corridor bag in hand.

'I've got my stuff. See you later. Don't worry about food, I've got something in, I'll cook for us both later.' He swung past her and turned as he reached the head of the stairs.

'Don't be late back, I'm doing something special.' Then he disappeared at speed. There was a curious air of barely suppressed excitement about him that awoke all her previous misgivings but banishing them determinedly she went into her sitting room to collect the various things she needed. Before she left, for reasons that she did not try to explain to herself, she went into the spare room and stripped off the sheets, fetching fresh linen from the airing cupboard and remaking the bed. She cleaned the small bathroom, scrubbing the bath and basin and meticulously cleaning the lavatory finishing off with a lavish application of bleach then she unpacked her bag, putting out her toiletries on the dressing table and in the bathroom and hanging clothes in the wardrobe. Half of her knew she was being foolish and it would all have to be moved again tomorrow but somehow it was immensely important to claim ownership, if only temporarily, of this room and clear every sign of Simon out of it. When she had finished she looked around with satisfaction and then glanced at her watch. She had better get a move on or she would not get everything done in town before the bank and her insurance brokers closed.

As she left the room and closed the door she wished very much that there was a lock on it but, of course, there wasn't. What need had there ever been for such a thing? Driving into town Simon's last words came into her mind: 'I'll cook... something special...' For two pins I wouldn't go back this evening. I could drive up the coast to Robbie's, I know he'd fit me in, she thought. But as she parked the car and walked towards the bank she knew she wouldn't do it. That's the curse of being brought up with good manners, she thought, half amused and half exasperated with herself. The last thing I want is a tête-à-tête dinner with Simon but I can't let him get it all ready and not turn up. Perhaps I can use this occasion to get it home to him that all these ideas he has are founded on nothing except his imagination and he must make his own new life away from me.

By five thirty she had completed everything she had to do and started back but the closer she got to home the more slowly she drove. I don't think I can face this after all, she thought. I'll phone and say I've been delayed and some problems have come up that I need to see David about, that I'll eat out and see him tomorrow.

With a huge feeling of relief she pulled into the side of the road and tried first her home number. When her own answer phone clicked in she disconnected and tried

186

Simon's mobile. The tinny voice informed her that the person she was calling was not available and she punched the 'off' button fiercely in frustration. First one and then the other and also, in desperation, the restaurant number but there was no answer. Eventually she pulled out and, driving into the village, went into the pub. Duncan greeted her with cries of exaggerated joy but real affection, seating her at the bar and pouring her some wine before she could stop him. When she protested he placed it firmly in front of her and told her not to be stupid. 'One glass, sweetie, and you're ten minutes from home. And when was the last time you saw "plod" out here? Drink up and relax. What a time you've been having, my darling! Tell me all about it. Do they know who started the fire?'

Laughing, protesting but feeling hugely comforted by his genuine warmth and concern she did as he said and as the bar gradually filled up and people came up to her, all expressing their own shock and friendly interest in what had happened, she did truly relax. While refusing any more wine she accepted a couple more of her usual lime and sodas and finally looking at her watch was rather aghast to see that it was almost eight o'clock. She tried all the phone numbers again but getting no reply she reluctantly decided that she had better go home. As she closed the door on the light and laughter inside she felt suddenly very cold and shivered. The prospect of the next hour or two made her feel as though she had a puddle of ice where her stomach should have been but there was no help for it, she must go back. As she turned into the drive she thought, 'I needn't have this out tonight. I'll just have dinner and go to bed and wait 'til Tessa comes back. I'll do it then.' Deciding this she realised that what she was really feeling was fear, but of what? How ridiculous. What could he really do?

As she walked towards the house she noticed that there were no lights on anywhere. None in her sitting room, which faced the front, the whole house was blank and dark. She could see the restaurant curtains were closed and they had certainly been open earlier but she was too intent on her own thoughts to consider whether this was odd.

As she reached the door it swung open and Simon stood there, swaying slightly, a glass in his hand. Looking into his face she went cold with shock. He was obviously violently angry and also drunk, which was all the more frightening because she had never known him drink more than moderately and never seen him even tipsy.

'Where the bloody hell have you been? I've been waiting for hours.'

He grabbed hold of her arm and pulled her inside slamming the door behind her and pushing her up the passage. As he did so she heard the grate of the key in the lock and turning saw him thrust the key into his trouser pocket.

'What are you doing, Simon?' In fear and shock her anger flared. 'How dare you lock me in? Give me that key.'

'Shut up!' It was almost a screech and sobered her immediately. 'Go upstairs.'

She stood stock still.

'What?'

'You heard me. Go upstairs. Now.'

Hester didn't move.

'No.'

She received a shove in her back so violent that she almost fell. 'Do as I say. Go upstairs.'

She turned around but he was so close behind her that she was forced to back onto the first step. Her heart was hammering in her chest but she forced herself to try to speak calmly.

'Simon, what's going on? Why are you being like this? I'm sorry I'm so late. I did try to reach you to tell you I was delayed but I couldn't get a reply.'

'All the phones are off.'

'What do you mean, "off"?'

'We don't want to be disturbed.' He was watching her face and something in its pallor and horrified expression seemed to pierce his anger and his own expression softened.

He reached towards her but she flinched and moved away, stumbling backwards up two more stairs.

'I'm sorry, Hester—there's no need to look so frightened, it's not like I'm going to hurt you. I suppose I was upset because you were so late and I've been planning it all so carefully. Look, you go and have a bath and change and we'll have dinner. I want this to be the most special night you've ever had.'

'I don't want to bath and change.'

Her voice sounded childish to her own ears so she tried again.

'I'm sorry, Simon, I know I was late but honestly, I'm absolutely shattered. Look, let's just have dinner and I'll get off to bed. It's been a long day.'

She saw his face harden again and he took a deep swallow from his glass. 'You have to have a bath. It's all part of the plan. I've laid out your dress on the bed. You'll see.'

Hester swallowed. The sudden switching of mood left her disorientated. It seemed that there was no getting around going upstairs so she turned and made her way up followed so closely she could feel his breath on her neck.

As she entered the spare room she had to accustom her eyes to the dim light. There were candles on all available surfaces and the air was heavy with a sickly floral scent. She saw that something was spread out on the duvet and she went across to look. Her blood truly ran cold.

She looked up at Simon standing at the foot of the bed, his eyes on her face and an odd, self-satisfied smirk lifting his mouth.

She swallowed but her voice came out in a croak.

'I sent this dress to a charity shop years and years ago. You took it for me with a lot of other things when I was...' Her voice faded away as she watched him lean forward smoothing the soft silky folds with the sort of delicacy with which a man might stroke a woman's skin. Her own skin crawled.

'I couldn't let it go. How could you just throw it away?' He continued stroking and drawing it through his fingers, his eyes fixed on it. 'You were wearing this the first time I saw you. Father brought me back from the station and there you were, standing in front of the fire, waiting for me, wearing this.'

He gave it a final lingering caress and straightened up, his eyes meeting hers.

All the anger had gone from his face and it was as if somehow it had been wiped clean of his thirty-four years, leaving it without lines or character, like that of a child with clear, untroubled blue eyes and a small, happy smile.

Hester had never been so frightened in her life.

She stood quietly, waiting.

'So now you see why you must have a bath and then put on your dress. You do see now, don't you?' He waited expectantly. She opened her mouth but no sound came out. She shook her head dumbly.

He said patiently, 'You have your bath and put on your dress and we start from the beginning again. Now do you see?' He started to walk towards her but she couldn't move. She was rooted to the spot as if her mind was working so hard to make sense of what was happening that her body had no energy to move.

Very gently he uncoiled the knot of hair at the back of her head, removing the clip and letting it fall around her shoulders. He ran his fingers down it, loosening the strands until it framed her face and then stood back.

'There!' he said with satisfaction. 'That's how it looked. But you must wash it when you bath. It must be clean and shining and curly, like it was on that day.'

Moving the dress gently to one side he lay down on the bed, placing his empty glass on the side table and folding his arms behind his head.

'Now, go and have your bath, I'll just wait here.' He picked up the glass again and held it out to her, smiling impishly. 'You can bring me a refill from what I've put in the bathroom.'

She took the glass between numb fingers and went across to the bathroom door.

Scented candles had been placed on every available surface and in the confined space and steamy warmth of the little room the smell was almost unbearable. On the stool stood an ice bucket holding a full bottle of champagne with a silver top on it. As if in a dream she filled Simon's glass and started back with it but his voice stooped her.

'No. Bring one for yourself as well.'

Obediently she went back and filled the empty glass beside the bucket and brought them carefully to the bed. He patted the duvet beside him and as she sat down he clinked his glass against hers.

'To our wonderful new life together. There's no one now to get in the way, nothing to come between us. To us.'

Hester took a tiny sip, which ran down her throat like acid. She cleared her throat, improvising rapidly.

'I don't want to spoil your plans but I'm expecting Frank any time now. He's popping in for a drink.'

Simon took a deep swallow and lay back on the pillows. A most peculiar smile flickered across his face.

'I don't think so. I don't think Frank will be coming again.'

'What do you mean?' She was sharp with alarm.

'It's not important. He just won't be coming. Now go and have your bath.'

191

The gentle note had gone and the hectoring tone was back.

Feeling more helpless than she had ever felt in her life, Hester took off her coat and started to collect clean underwear from the drawer.

A voice from the bed said, 'Wear those pearl earrings I bought you for Christmas and the pearl bracelet.'

Like an automaton Hester opened the top drawer of her dressing table and reached in for her jewellery box. Her hand closed around something small and hard. Her heart stopped. Her old mobile phone. Two weeks previously she had treated herself to a new one, an all-singing all-dancing one with integral camera because she had temporarily lost the old one. When she had found it again she had simply put it away in this drawer. She pulled the drawer fully open, drew out the necklace and earrings and at the same time stuffed the phone into the handful of underwear, and closing the drawer started towards the bathroom.

She began to close the door when the voice spoke again.

'Don't shut it, I might need to come and get some more champagne.'

He was slightly slurring his words now and, internally, she shuddered.

She turned.

'Allow me some privacy, Simon, I want to go to the loo. Nobody is allowed to watch me do that. I'll open it when I've finished.' She closed the door firmly and leant against it trying to steady her breathing but her mind raced. This was her only chance to make contact with anyone before... before what? Her mind shrank away from what she couldn't bear to contemplate.

Police? No, how could she explain and anyway he would hear her speak. Frantically she tried to order her thoughts, crossing the bathroom and sitting on the lavatory seat, clutching her lifeline in slippery fingers. Tessa. Tessa was waiting for a call so would check her phone for messages. It was her only chance. She pressed the 'On' button. The battery showed only one bar and she didn't dare waste time checking her credit. Calling up the message box she selected 'write message' and started to text. 'SOS COME NOW SIMON MAD V SCARED PLS PLS COME NOW H.'

She selected Tessa's number and pressed 'Send'. She watched the little envelope flashing and prayed that there would be enough credit and battery power to send the message.

Suddenly she heard the bed creak. In panic she fumbled for the flush handle, pulled at her clothes, stuffed the mobile in the middle and bundled the whole pile into the clothes basket. She pulled the door slightly ajar and got quickly into the bath.

It was only tepid so she ran some water out and tipping in a generous amount of foaming bath oil she ran more hot water so that it was almost at the top. Sliding down under the bubbles which completely concealed her she breathed out for what felt like the first time since entering the bathroom and closed her eyes.

There was nothing else to be done now. She had no idea whether the text had been sent. She lay in the warmth hoping desperately that Tessa would pick up the message and realise the urgency. The only other thing to do was to try and make each stage of the evening last as long as possible and delay the inevitable ending. It was useless to pretend to herself any longer. Simon believed himself to be in love with her and tonight he planned to seduce her and had managed to delude himself into believing that she was a willing partner. What terrified her most was that she felt quite sure that his mental balance was hanging by a hair—if not already completely overturned. Why had she not picked up the signs, as looking back they had been so clear to see? Sliding down further into the water she closed her eyes. All she could do now was pray.

Chapter 19

Tessa sat at the kitchen table moodily watching Bunny stack the dishwasher. She glanced up at the kitchen clock for the umpteenth time and sighed. Bunny regarded her with a glimmer of sympathy.

'You'd better get used to it, my girl, this is what it'll be like, married to a vet.'

Tessa sighed again. 'I know, I know. It's just it's my last evening and I had hoped… Oh well. Once this new chap gets more experienced it will be better. At the moment poor Tim's between a rock and a hard place. His dad doesn't do any evening call outs and Nigel can't be left on his own with anything too complicated.'

'Why don't you have your dinner now? Tim can have his whenever he does arrive.'

'No, I'll wait. I'll try him on the mobile again, but if he's in the middle of the foaling he won't answer.'

But as she picked up her phone she saw that there was a message. Something in her silence caught Bunny's attention.

'Something wrong?' she asked sharply.

'Yes.' Tessa, answered slowly. 'I think there is. Very wrong.'

She repeated the message aloud and Bunny frowned. 'What's all that about?

She sounds terrified. Try phoning her.'

'Yes, of course.' But after several minutes of fruitless trying she laid the phone down and sat staring in front of her.

'Well, what are you going to do?' Bunny demanded.

'I wish I could get hold of Tim but that's hopeless. I'll just have to go.'

'What, now? On your own? I don't think that's a good idea.'

'I must. I know why she's contacted me. Nobody else

would realise how serious this is. She must be so frightened. God knows what he's doing.'

She got up, picking up bag and car keys and shrugging on her jacket.

'Wait a minute.' Bunny held her arm. 'You really think he's that dangerous?'

'Yes, I do. I'm damn certain he caused that girl's death one way or another. He's utterly obsessed with Hester and I think he's completely lost the plot. I must go.'

Bunny held on to her arm. 'Surely there's someone down there you could get hold of?'

'There isn't. I haven't got any numbers for the staff. They're all in the restaurant phone.'

Bunny shook her arm. 'What about that architect fellah, David isn't it?'

'No not his either. Why would I?'

'Well perhaps you should call the police.'

'On the strength of a text message? They haven't a clue what's been going on. They're never interested until something's happened and then it's too late. I'll keep trying Tim from the car but the calving could go on all night if there are complications.'

She pushed Bunny's hand off her arm. 'It's no good Bun, I've got to go. We're wasting time. Nobody else will understand.'

'Well you're not going on your own. I'm coming with you.'

Tessa stared back at her dumbfounded for a few seconds then nodded her head.

'All right,' she said briskly, 'you come. I just hope we get there in time.'

As they joined the motorway Bunny broke the silence.

'You said "in time". What exactly are you afraid of?'

'I'm not sure,' Tessa said grimly. 'I only know that Hester would never have sent that message unless she was badly frightened. You keep checking to see if there's another message.'

'How long will it take us?'

'About two hours from now. Luckily it's pretty quiet tonight, not much traffic. Let's hope there are no "plods" around because I'll get a speeding ticket for sure.'

'Good thing you brought your dad's car then.' Bunny switched on the radio and settled back into the passenger seat of the Jaguar.

As the big car ate up the miles Tessa's anxiety grew. She drove with fierce and silent concentration but suddenly she said urgently to Bunny, 'Turn that up, quick.'

The announcer's voice said, '…and the body has now been identified as that of Frank Davis. His boat had been noticed by another local fisherman as not having moved all day so he went to investigate and found no one on board. He alerted the coastguard service and after a search of the area divers were sent down in the immediate proximity and the body was discovered and brought up. The police are investigating…'

'Oh my God, poor Hester.' Tessa's voice was a whisper and Bunny sat bolt upright.

'What's the matter? Who's this Davis?'

'A very close friend of Hester's. Well more than a friend. She'll be terribly upset.'

Tessa's foot went down to the floor and the needle crept up to ninety-eight miles per hour.

Bunny glanced at it and closed her eyes.

* * *

With his feet up on the sofa and his Chinese takeaway balanced on his stomach Adrian was idly watching the television but concentrating on not dropping the noodles on his chest on their way to his mouth. The sound was turned low but suddenly his attention was caught. An eerily familiar coastline appeared behind the news announcer's head with a small fishing boat just above his left ear. Noodles forgotten, Adrian pressed the remote and heard the announcer's voice.

'...and the body has been identified as Frank Davis, a local fisherman. He had apparently gone out in the early hours to check his lobster pots and at sometime between then and four o'clock this afternoon when the coastguard was called he is presumed to have fallen overboard. It is not yet known whether foul play is suspected.'

The rest of the news passed Adrian by as he sat motionless trying to grasp the implications of what he had heard. The last time he had seen the outline of those cliffs was at three o'clock the previous morning and that little boat or one uncannily similar had crossed the bay in front of him as he crouched in the shadows. Then Simon had appeared, disappeared and then reappeared approximately an hour later in that same bay. Another half an hour passed until very slowly he picked up his mobile and pressed the speed dial for his paper.

'Hi, it's Adrian, put me through to the Night Editor would you?'

* * *

In bathing, drying her hair, making up her face and dressing, Hester had managed to drag out another hour.

Now his plan was unfolding on its ordained course Simon seemed content to lie on the bed, sipping his wine and watching her as she moved around the room and sat at her dressing table. When there was nothing further she could think of to lengthen the process of getting ready she hooked on the earrings, clasped the bracelet and stood up.

'Well, Simon, what about this dinner you've promised me. I'm starving.'

To her own ears her voice sounded more briskly nanny-ish than lover-like but Simon did not appear to notice and carrying the remains of the champagne in its bucket he led the way downstairs.

When they entered the restaurant she could see why the curtains had been drawn. He had pushed several tables back from the middle leaving one in splendid isolation with just a chair each side. Perfectly laid with candles and flowers and gleaming silver and white linen it looked like a stage set. As he drew out her chair for her to sit she could see that he had indeed provided a superb dinner. Some sort of paté, prettily garnished, cold dressed lobster in its shell, a spun sugar and cream dessert, a cheese board and two bottles of wine, one red, one white.

'Good heavens, Simon, there's enough here for an army. We'll never get through it.'

The self-satisfied smirk she had come to dread reappeared.

'I told you it was going to be special. Tuck in.'

To her own surprise Hester found she was quite hungry but once the edge had been taken off her appetite by the paté she found it increasingly difficult to eat and Simon began to look impatient as she toyed with the lobster, pushing it around the plate and eating tiny pieces with a pretence of enjoyment. In desperation she started to drink some of the wine, sipping it slowly to make it last, her mind still racing around the same track. How to get away? How to stop this horrible evening reaching its allotted end? Unused to drinking much, the wine began to have an effect, blurring the edges of her panic and almost inducing a false euphoria.

As Simon poured her third glass she felt an hysterical bubble of laughter rise inside her. Perhaps if she got completely drunk she wouldn't be able to get up the stairs. Perhaps she would pass out and that would stop him. Or perhaps it wouldn't. Would having sex with an unconscious woman count as necrophilia? No, that was dead people wasn't it. The bubble was in her throat, at any moment she would laugh out loud. Her blurred gaze fixed on Simon's face and she saw that he was frowning.

'I think perhaps you've had enough wine.' He moved the half-full glass to his own side of the table and poured some water into an empty glass.

'Here, have some of this.'

'I want some more wine.' Her voice sounded strange in her own ears, sulky and childish again. She tried a different tack.

'Really, Simon, it's very good wine. I'd like my glass back.'

He was still frowning, intent on her face.

'No. I don't like you like this. You never get drunk. I won't have it.'

She made a clumsy movement and the glass of water tipped over and rolled off the table on to the floor and shattered.

'Oh dear, look what I've done,' she giggled foolishly and bent down to gather up the pieces.

'Leave it,' he said harshly. 'Just leave it. I'll pour you some more water.'

Her napkin slid off her knee as she started to straighten up. She leant down again to pick it up and felt a sharp point prick her finger. Folding the napkin round the shard of glass, she sat up and placed them on her lap.

'You haven't eaten much lobster.' His voice was angry now.

She blinked at him. 'It was lovely, I think I made rather a pig of myself with the paté. I'd like to try some of that gorgeous looking pudding.'

It was in fact the last thing she wanted. The combination of rich food, too much wine, the stuffy overheated warmth of the room and the curdling fear in the pit of her stomach was making her feel sick but she must try to continue dragging out this nightmare meal. She managed a surreptitious glance at her watch. Almost two hours since she had sent her message. But had Tessa received it? And if so, had she picked it up? There was no knowing.

She slowly forced down a minute portion of the sticky sweet dessert and then helped herself to a morsel of cheese and a spray of grapes. She knew this could not last much longer and the cold fear spread until she felt as if her whole body was encased in it.

Simon had given up any effort at eating but was drinking steadily, his blue eyes fixed on her face, clear and glittering with strange brilliance. He had been talking fairly continuously throughout the meal, outlining his plans for their joint future, which became more grandiose and far-fetched as the evening progressed. He appeared completely unaware of her total lack of response and his assumption of her complete agreement to everything he projected made her chillingly aware of his detachment from reality. But now he had fallen silent, his gaze roving from her face to her shoulders and breasts, sharply outlined in the clinging silk dress, which was uncomfortably tight twenty years on from when she had last worn it. Abruptly he put his glass down on the table and stood up.

'Time to go up, don't you think?'

'Oh no,' she protested, her voice rising, 'I'd like some more cheese. It's really delicious.'

'It'll still be here tomorrow,' he said dryly. 'Come on, Hester, don't you think we've waited long enough? I've been very patient. I've had years of being patient.'

He bent towards her, his voice beginning to rise. 'What is the matter with you, Hester? We know it's what we both want, we needn't wait any longer. There is nothing to stop us being together, nothing.'

Hester fought the urge to pull away from his relentless gaze. 'Simon, it still doesn't feel right,' she said desperately. 'So many years of treating you like a son, that's how I've always thought of you, I can't just suddenly change.'

He stood over her looking down.

'I've never thought of you as my mother. I fell in love with you the moment I saw you, I know that now.'

'You were only eleven years old,' she protested.

'What's that got to do with it? I've never cared about anyone else and neither have you. It's always been about us, you know it has. It was just a case of waiting for the right time. And this is the right time so stop being difficult and come upstairs.' He caught hold of her arm, pulling her out of her chair.

Her face only inches from his, her stomach churning, she said frantically, 'I'm sure you must have realised Frank is my lover. We've been lovers for years so how can you say I've never loved anyone else.'

The stinging blow to her cheek snapped her head back.

'Don't dare to say that, don't ever say his name again. He's gone. Jennifer's gone. No one can come between us. They were nothing, less than nothing. Just passing the time until you and I could be together. We have no need of anyone else. Ever.'

There was a deathly silence. Hester heard herself whisper, 'You killed her didn't you? You pushed her off that cliff? What's happened to Frank? What have you done to him?'

'I've told you,' he said impatiently, 'neither of them need trouble us again. Now, upstairs.'

Still holding her arm he started towards the door. On leaden feet she walked beside him.

When they reached the bedroom, still pulling her along he went to the bed and sat down.

'Stand in front of me,' he commanded.

Unable to think she obediently did as she was told.

'Closer,' he said, 'stand between my knees.'

Slowly, she moved to stand between his legs. She could hear his breathing quicken and deepen as he reached up and started to unbutton the bodice of her dress. Frozen with disgust and misery she stood motionless, a useless litany repeating itself over and over in her head, 'Tessa, please come, Tessa, please come.'

She stared over Simon's head trying to divorce herself from what was happening below, blindly repeating her mantra. She felt the dress slither away over her hips to the floor, she felt his hands fumbling with the hooks of her bra and the weight of her breasts as they were released then his fingers stroking and kneading and lastly his lips as they fastened around her nipples and a sobbing moan as his hands pulled at the delicate lace of her pants, dragging them down towards her knees.

An uncontrollable shudder shook her and her hands clenched. A sharp pain seared her right palm and in a moment of clarity she realised she still held the shard of glass. She thought of the last man to touch her and the tears started to stream down her face. Without a thought she raised her hand and dragged it down the side of his face and neck.

With a sickening grunt his head jerked back and his eyes met hers. He clapped his hand to his face and brought it away, staring unbelievingly at his bloody palm.

He looked up at her blankly.

'What have you done?' His voice was a thread. 'Why? Why have you done this?'

The peculiar spell which seemed to have sapped her will was broken. She stepped back aware of the door behind her.

'I told you, Simon, I can't do this. It's all wrong. You wouldn't listen. It feels like…' she struggled for the words '…like incest. You have to stop.'

She was almost at the door now reaching behind her for the handle but she was not quick enough. He was off the bed and holding her in a tight embrace. Swinging her around he threw her onto the bed. He was shouting, almost screaming, the blood pouring from the cut, soaking into his white shirt.

'How could you do this? How can you say it's wrong? How could you say anything so filthy, you're mine, you're mine, you've always been mine, now it's the right time, now, tonight, it's the right time the perfect time...'

Now he was sobbing, incoherent phrases while he held her down on the bed, his hand at her throat while he tore at his trousers with the other. He kicked them away and then his full weight was on top of her, his knee forcing her legs apart, his mouth trying to fasten on hers as she thrashed from side to side under him. Somehow the shard of glass had gone, probably somewhere on the floor. She had no defence; he was stronger than she was.

She screamed, 'No! No! No!' over and over but she knew it was no use and then—nothing. Just the dead weight of Simon's body, inert, still. The next moment the weight was gone, rolled onto the floor and Tessa's appalled face was looking down at her, comforting arms lifting her up, and behind her Bunny's wrinkled old mask registering equal horror.

'My poor love, my poor, poor love. What has he done to you? Where are you hurt? So much blood.'

'It's not mine, it's his,' Hester said weakly. 'I cut him.' And then the dam burst: great racking sobs shuddering through her body, tears streaming, every part of her shaking.

Tessa fetched the towelling robe from the bathroom and wrapped her in it, switching on the electric blanket and tucking the duvet around her.

'Bunny, can you find the kitchen and make tea. Strong and sweet.'

'Right.' As Bunny turned to go she gave Simon's inert form a far from gentle kick. 'What are we going to do with this rubbish?'

'Rubbish is about right,' said Tessa grimly. 'We need to

204

put him somewhere safe until the police come. Hester's got an office at the end of the corridor. It's the only room with a lock on it. We'll put him in there. Hopefully he won't come around before they get here.'

Covering him with his trousers, together they dragged the unconscious man up the passage and locked him in the tiny room. As Bunny descended the stairs to the kitchen Tessa went back to Hester. The racking sobs were dying away but massive shudders still shook her and she shivered continuously.

Tessa sat next to her and silently held her hand until gradually she became quieter. Eventually she asked in a thread of a voice, 'What happened? How did it stop?'

'Bunny hit him over the head with that pottery bowl from the table in the hall. It weighs a ton and it didn't even break.'

'Where… where is he now?'

'Don't worry, he's lying unconscious in your office. He can stay there until the police come. If you're OK for a minute or two I'll go and ring them.'

Hester clutched her. 'Oh no. No police. I can't face it.'

Tessa stared at her. 'Hester, he's severely assaulted you, he tried to rape you. In fact…' She stopped. Hester shook her head in response.

Tessa spoke more softly. 'Hester, you have to report this, he's very dangerous. I feel all the more sure that he had something to do with that girl's death and…' She stopped again.

'And what?'

'Nothing. But you must hand him over, you know you must. He's completely lost it, you'll never be safe.'

There was a long silence. Eventually Hester whispered, 'I think he's done something to Frank.'

Tessa shifted uncomfortably.

'I wasn't going to tell you this until you were feeling a bit stronger but it was on the car radio coming down.

Frank's boat was discovered, unattended, by his lobster pots and this evening they fished a body out of the water. It was his. No immediate evidence of foul play. It looks like he fell overboard and drowned.'

Hester said very quietly, 'He couldn't swim. He'd never learnt. If he fell into deep water he wouldn't have had a chance.'

'Well, we can only hope that someone may have seen something that can shed some light on it. Now I must phone the police, mustn't I?'

Another silence then Hester sighed.

'Yes, I suppose you must. But the thought of going through it with them...' She fell silent and a shudder ran through her.

'I know, but I'll be here and I can tell them the end bit that I saw. Chin up, sweetheart, it'll all soon be over.'

Bunny came in with the tea and Tessa went out to phone. She was back in a few minutes. They're coming straight away. They'll be about twenty minutes.'

As they sat there in silence drinking the tea the sound of a car engine starting up brought Tessa to her feet.

'That's the Porsche. Bloody hell, he must have got out.'

She flew out into the corridor to see the office door still firmly locked. Down the stairs she went like the wind and out into the car park to see the Porsche tail lights disappearing round the bend. She looked up at the office window to see it wide open and the overflow pipe from the guttering hanging away from the wall. She went slowly back upstairs.

'He's gone all right but he won't get far, they'll have his description and car reg straight away. I'll phone them and tell them what's happened.'

When she had finished she said, 'There's a car still on its way to interview you but he won't get very far along these lanes. They're sure to put up road blocks, it would only need two.'

She spoke confidently but across Hester's head she cast Bunny a look of deep concern.

Silence descended again, there seemed to be nothing useful to say but after about half an hour Hester said tentatively, 'They're being rather a long time, don't you think?'

Tessa glanced at her watch. 'It's certainly a long twenty minutes but I imagine catching him is a top priority.'

Another half an hour crept past but at last they heard a car turning in and with a grim smile of relief Tessa ran down to meet them. She was some time downstairs and when she came back she was followed by both a policeman and woman. Tessa came over to the bed and took Hester's hand between both her own.

'Hester, there's no easy way to tell you this, love. There's been an accident. Simon must have been driving like a maniac. The police were rounding the corner and they saw the Porsche flying over the edge of the cliff.'

Hester sat up.

'Is he…' Her voice failed.

The police woman stepped forward. 'I'm afraid so, ma'am. The car caught fire as it went down. He didn't have a chance.' Tessa gripped the cold clenched fists.

'It's over, Hester. It's finished.'

Epilogue

Four weeks later.

The car drew in at the front of the restaurant. Tim got out of the driving seat opening the car door for the two women.

'You carry on in, I'll bring your bags.'

Hester unlocked the door and stood there for a moment. Tessa touched her arm. 'Are you OK?'

Hester smiled at her. 'Yes, I'll be fine. It's just, I haven't been back since Frank's funeral, it'll take some adjustment.'

'I know. I wish you'd let me stay, at least for a day or two. I don't think you should be alone yet.'

Hester did not immediately answer. They went to the sitting room and Hester smiled again as she walked across to the window.

'Dear Betty. She's done a grand job. Everything shining and fresh flowers everywhere. She is a gem.'

She turned to Tessa. 'It's wonderful of you to want to stay but you have done enough, you and Bunny and your family. I've had a lovely week with you and you've seen me through all the worst bits. Now I need to pick up the threads again and you need to get back to your own life.'

'And you're going to keep the restaurant closed for the time being?'

'Yes. There would be too many thrill-seekers coming just to look at me rather than eat my food. I've got enough in the bank to manage, so don't worry any more.'

Tim loomed in the doorway. 'Everything in. What now?'

Hester smiled affectionately at him. 'Now you are off the hook, my dears. Off you go. I'm fine. I'll take a walk down to the beach, I think. I miss my sea when I've been away.'

'If you're sure,' Tessa said doubtfully.

'I'm sure.' She put her arms around Tessa in a long,

hard hug. 'Truly, I can never thank you enough for all you've done. You know you'll both be welcome to come and stay whenever you like for as long as you want. I'll really miss you but life must go on.'

She kissed Tim's cheek and made shooing motions. 'Go on. Go!'

She followed them downstairs and as they turned to the car she went towards the cliff path, waving as she disappeared.

* * *

They walked over and watched as she went down, disappearing briefly under the overhang and appearing again on the sand. She walked a little way and then sat down on a rock gazing out to sea.

Tim draped an arm around Tessa's shoulders.

'Come on, hon. You can't nanny her forever.'

Tessa heaved a sigh. 'I know. She just looks so small and lonely sitting there. She's lost so much weight, she's kind of shrunk.'

'I'm hardly surprised with all she's been through but she'll survive. She's a tough woman.'

They turned towards the car and at that moment a taxi appeared at the top of the drive and drew to a stop beside their own car. The driver got out and opening the rear door helped a man out from the back. He straightened up and looked about him. Tessa stared at the tall figure, the craggy profile and the shock of grey hair.

'I don't believe it, Tim, I'm sure that's Peter Armitage. You know, the correspondent who was shot in Iraq. He's a friend of Hester's. I wonder how he knew she'd be here.'

As the man started to walk towards them they could see he was limping and one arm was hanging stiffly. He smiled as he reached them.

'You must be friends of Hester's. At a guess you are

Tessa and Tim.' He held out his good arm and they shook hands.

Tessa asked, 'How did you know about us?'

'I've been talking to Hester over the past few days but I haven't been fit enough to come and see her. As you see I still can't drive. Is she in the house?' Tessa pointed towards the cliff.

'No, she's on the beach.'

He walked over and looked down.

'I may have to wait for her to come up. I'm not sure I'll make the path,' Tim moved forward.

'I'll give you a hand, sir, if you want to go. I could walk in front and you could hang on.'

Peter Armitage regarded his massive frame and smiled his famously attractive smile.

'I think that would be safe. Thanks.'

Tessa watched the slow descent and Peter appeared on the sand walking towards Hester's oblivious figure. As if an invisible string had been tightened Hester turned her head. For a moment she was motionless and then jumping off the rock she started to run up the beach. Peter stopped, his good arm held wide and as she reached him the two figures melted together, Hester's arm around his neck pulling his head to hers.

Tessa watched, unaware of tears running down her cheeks. Tim reappeared beside her, peering into her face, his own alight with loving amusement. He wiped the tears with his finger and kissed her nose.

'You old softie. It's going to be fine now. Come along.' He slipped his arm around her shoulders and started to urge her gently towards the car. Looking over her shoulder at the two motionless figures she said anxiously, 'I hope he's going to be kind to her.'

'I don't think you need to worry,' Tim stopped, hesitating for a moment then continued, 'When we got to the bottom of the cliff he had to stop to get his breath back. He was watching Hester and he just said, "Tim, I have been such a bloody fool. I've wasted so much time. I hope she's going to let me make it up to her. Wish me luck", and off he went.'

Tessa stared hard at the top button of Tim's shirt and then looked up into his face.

'That's all right then,' she said and smiled. 'Let's go home.'

***